H. E. Bates was born in 1905 at Rushden in Northampton-
shire and was educated at Kettering Grammar School.
He worked as a journalist and clerk on a local news-
paper before publishing his first book, *The Two Sisters*,
when he was twenty. In the next fifteen years he acquired
a distinguished reputation for his stories about English
country life. During the Second World War, he was a
Squadron Leader in the R.A.F. and some of his stories of
service life, *The Greatest People in the World* (1942), *How Sleep
the Brave* (1943) and *The Face of England* (1953) were written
under the pseudonym of 'Flying Officer X'. His subsequent
novels of Burma, *The Purple Plain* and *The Jacaranda Tree*, and
of India, *The Scarlet Sword*, stemmed directly or indirectly
from his war experience in the Eastern theatre of war.

In 1958 his writing took a new direction with the
appearance of *The Darling Buds of May*, the first of the popular
Larkin family novels, which was followed by *A Breath
of French Air*, *When the Green Woods Laugh* and *Oh! To Be
in England* (1963). His autobiography appeared in three
volumes, *The Vanished World* (1969), *The Blossoming World*
(1971) and *The World in Ripeness* (1972). His last works
included the novel, *The Triple Echo* (1971) and a collection of
short stories, *The Song of the Wren* (1972). Perhaps one of his
most famous works of fiction is the best-selling novel *Fair
Stood the Wind for France* (1944). H. E. Bates also wrote
miscellaneous works on gardening, essays on country life,
several plays including *The Day of Glory* (1945); *The Modern
Short Story* (1941) and a story for children, *The White Admiral*
(1968). His works have been translated into 16 languages and
a posthumous collection of his stories, *The Yellow Meads of
Asphodel*, appeared in 1976.

H. E. Bates was awarded the C.B.E. in 1973 and died in
January 1974. He was married in 1931 and had four children.

H. E. BATES

THE NATURE OF LOVE

THREE SHORT NOVELS

PENGUIN BOOKS
IN ASSOCIATION WITH
MICHAEL JOSEPH

Penguin Books Ltd, Harmondsworth, Middlesex, England
Viking Penguin Inc., 40 West 23rd Street, New York, New York 10010, U.S.A.
Penguin Books Australia Ltd, Ringwood, Victoria, Australia
Penguin Books Canada Ltd, 2801 John Street, Markham, Ontario, Canada L3R 1B4
Penguin Books (N.Z.) Ltd, 182-190 Wairau Road, Auckland 10, New Zealand

First published by Michael Joseph 1953
Published in Penguin Books 1958
Reprinted 1984, 1985

Printed and bound in Great Britain by
Cox & Wyman Ltd, Reading
Set in Garamond

To

W. SOMERSET MAUGHAM

CONTENTS

DULCIMA   9

THE GRASS GOD   67

THE DELICATE NATURE   127

DULCIMA

I

SHE was a short girl, thick in the back, with stout legs covered by brownish cotton stockings and flat feet by big sloppy shoes. Her hands were large and coarse and her straight dark hair hung down over her solid cheek-bones in uncombed strands. In twenty-seven years she had never had much time, as she remembered it, to bother with her hair.

Every afternoon she pushed an old hoodless pram, with a baby in it, up the hillside, through high woods of beeches, under greening crags of chalk, to where the road ended by Parker's farm. The woods were so large that there were always new-blown branches of beechwood lying on the slopes of dry copper leaves and she always loaded the pram with them, so that finally the baby lay almost buried under a crooked roof of boughs. When she pushed the pram up the road she thrust her head forward, making the big solid legs dig backwards and gain their power from the slope of the hill. When she went down the hill she thrust her legs forward, straining the front of her body outward, so that she could hold the load from running away. Sometimes after storms the woods were filled with a wreckage of broken branches and she felt greedy about it and piled the pram so high with them that she could hardly hold the weight of it back. Then she ran down the hill, pounding her thick legs on the road with lumbering stabs that filled the long high woods with clapping echoes.

She was very conscious of her legs; she had always been terribly aware of their ugliness. She was aware too of the coarseness of her hands. But she felt that she could have borne even the ugliness of the big squabby hands and the flabbiness of a face in which the lips were too thick and the eyes slightly out of proportion and the hair too coarse to bother with if only her legs had been tolerable. Every girl

9

wanted legs with some kind of shapeliness. There were things you could do to a plain or even an ugly face to make it more tolerable, even to make it attractive or striking or beautiful, and you could always put smooth new gloves on your hands. But she felt there was nothing you could do to change legs that were only lumps of fat hideously knotted with raised blue veins. They were something horrible, like a deformity, an affliction, you could not disguise.

She felt too that there were reasons why her legs had grown like that. She had never known the time when there was not a baby in the pram. She had never known the time when she was not slopping up the hill in her big flat shoes, pushing the pram, covering it with firewood, then pushing it down again. There seemed never to have been a time when she did not stand at the copper, pounding at clothes, or at the sink, washing dishes for a dozen people. She knew that these were the things that thickened and coarsened and twisted your legs into shapelessness, tying them with slaty and hideous veins. Standing and lugging and standing and pushing and standing on her own weight all day had destroyed the things she wanted to be most beautiful.

Her mother was a hollow-faced whining woman with meagre breasts that were like empty purses except when they filled briefly and fed another child. Her face was yellow with a haunted look. It was the look of someone trying to remember something – a pleasant thing or a comforting thing or the reason for something or the details of a lost intention. She seemed to be trying to recapture something. And over the years she had expressed the impossibility of recapture by giving her children proud and fancy names. They were called Rowena and Chalice and Spenser, and then Clarissa and Angela and Cassandra and Abigail, and even Magnolia and Sharon, two who had died.

The name of the eldest, the girl who pushed the pram, was Dulcima. Her father called her Dulce. It was her mother's way, in preservation of successive dreams, to call the children by their full names, with a kind of round, doting, stupid grandeur. But for her father it was Dulce.

It was Abb and Cass and Clar and Ange and even Ro and Spen. Her father, a man with cheeks fissured dark by long hours in brick kilns, had no time for names, for doting or for fanciful things. Work at the kiln seemed, after years, to have burnt the juices out of him, so that he was dry of kindliness. Shallow grey eyes were cemented into a head that had no colour. Even the diminutives of the names he used were not soft in effect. He rapped them out hard and chipped, like chisel blows.

'Drop that, Abb, else I'll git the strap. Stoppit, Cass – any more lip and I'll mark you. I'll mark you, by God I will.'

He was proud, as he said, to have them at a word.

'I want shoes,' she would say. 'I'm walking wet-foot now. I bin walking wet-foot for a week. Every day.'

'You'll git shoes, you'll git shoes. I ain't made o' shoes, am I?'

'Git shoes with what? They had a pair at the jumble and I hadn't a mite to bless myself with. Git shoes with what?'

'Dulcima, don't you urge your father. Don't you urge him like that –'

'Let him git me a pair o' shoes then. Let him stop Dulcing me all day long. Dulce this, Dulce that, where's Dulce? Let him stop Dulcing me and git me a pair o' shoes.'

'You'll git shoes, time enough, you'll git shoes.'

'Time enough for what? – I'll git shoes but it won't be here. I'll Dulce out o' here one o' these days. I'll Dulce out and git myself some shoes. I ain't a dog walking on my bare feet. I ain't a dog – I won't be treated like a dog.'

Like a dog, every afternoon, she pushed the pram through the beechwoods, up the hill. Like her mother, as she pressed forward on thick ugly legs, she became preoccupied with successive dreams: a dream of shoes, of a decent dress, a dream of some way to make her legs less hideous, of a time when she might wear white gloves on her hands.

2

Every Tuesday and Friday, market days, Parker came up the hill, driving a mud-stained open Ford with a trailer.

She did not think of this as an extraordinary thing. It happened so regularly and so often that she hardly noticed it. Always on those days, about the same time, she heard the clash of gears as Parker turned the corner and began to climb the hill through the beeches. She heard the echoed rattle of the worn-out Ford clashing up into the high cover of branches. She saw the car coming out of the lower woodland like a drugged and slightly crazy buffalo, nosing from side to side, lurching in heavy curves so that sometimes she had to pull the pram into the chalk verge until it was safely past her.

Every day too she saw the thin drunk-grey face of Parker as it went past without looking at her. In winter mud from the Ford splashed her cotton stockings and as spring came on white chalk dust was beaten up into her face. She showed no sign that these things irritated her. Sometimes she stood holding a broken branch in her hand, staring thoughtfully after Parker, watching him until, at last, the car lurched and disappeared through the gate of the farm.

On a day in late April Parker came up the hill faster than usual. She heard the car roaring up the road like an ancient and rickety train. She had just time to pull the pram into the verge before Parker went past her and the Ford, bouncing, hit the snake fence thirty yards beyond.

At first she did not move. She stood gripping the handle of the pram and watching Parker trying to get out of the car. She saw the drunk-grey face straining across the seats; the hands groping along the edges of the dusty car body for support.

She watched for some moments longer and then Parker fell out of the car. He hit the roadside face first and then turned over convulsively and lay still. At the same moment the car engine coughed in a back-fire that was like a pistol-shot and the sound woke the baby, so that it began to cry.

The sound of its crying startled her more than the crash had done and suddenly she found herself running forward, shouting:

'Mr Parker! Mr Parker! Are you all right, Mr Parker? Whatever has happened?'

After some moments Parker opened his eyes, saw her and tried to stand up. She watched him for some seconds shuddering on the raised edge of grass. Then he fell down on his face again. His black trilby hat had already fallen off and now she picked it up. It was covered with a white bloom of chalk dust and she began to brush it with her hands.

The inner rim of the hat, when she turned it over, seemed to be stuffed with paper: as if it were too big for the small skinny head of Parker, who had padded it to the right size.

Then she saw that this paper was not merely paper. It was in the form of many pound notes, neatly folded and packed tight inside the hat, under the greasy leather band.

'I'll get you home, Mr Parker,' she said. 'Mr Parker, I'll get you home.'

For some few seconds she was torn between the problem of Parker, the hat, and the crying baby. She solved it by leaving Parker where he was and taking the hat to the pram. Then she pushed the pram to the farm-gate, rocking it up and down so that the baby stopped its crying. Finally she pushed the hat behind the pillow and then came back to where Parker was.

He was still dazed as she lifted him up with stout arms and, in the same solid way as she pushed the pram up and down the hill, carried him to the house. His fall had left a long streak of blood on his left cheek and she said:

'Mr Parker, you might have killed yourself,' but Parker did not answer.

After she had dumped Parker into the big horsehair chair in the kitchen, her first thought was for the hat. She wheeled the pram to the kitchen door and then took out the hat and put it on the kitchen table.

'I'll git you a cuppa tea, Mr Parker,' she said. 'I'll wash

that blood off your face and git you a cuppa tea and you'll feel better.'

Again Parker did not answer. Nor did he seem to notice her movements about the kitchen as she filled the kettle, lighted the oil stove and got ready to bathe his face and make the tea. Cups and plates that Parker had used in the morning or the day before or even the day before that stood about the kitchen in odd places, on chairs, on the mantel-shelf, on window-ledges, in a sink filled with greasy stew-pans.

'You let yourself git into a rare mess,' she said and began to bathe his face.

Parker was a man of fifty-five and she had always thought of him, when she had thought of him at all, as being older than he was. Her first close look at his face did not change her mind. It was a face of small bone structure, narrow, with thin lips and sparse receding rabbit-coloured hair. A little frown of pained anxiety about something brought the small grey eyes rather close together.

Some time after she had washed his face Parker sat up. With stupefied eyes he looked glassily past her. He sat staring in this way until she brought him tea. She had the sense to bring it to him without a saucer and he sat with the cup grasped in both hands, staring, letting the tea fume up into his washed grey face without a word.

'Feel any better?' she said. 'You might have got yourself killed,' but again Parker did not answer.

While he drank the tea, she looked at the floor, splashed with grey hen-droppings, with mud and mud-straw from the yard and with old stray feathers; at the crockery lying on mantelpiece and window-sill and chairs; and at the colourless skeins of lace that had once been curtains; and she said:

'Don't nobody come in and give you a clean-up once in a while?'

He seemed to shake his head; and suddenly she felt in a clumsy way sorry for him: drunk, womanless, lost, unable to answer her.

'Well, it's time somebody did.' She pulled at her stockings that had slipped slightly down in concertina ruckles over her stout legs, but Parker did not notice them. 'If I git time to-morrow I'll come in and give you a bit of sweep-up. Not afore you want it either.'

Parker seemed to nod his head, still as if not seeing her properly, and after some moments she said, 'You take care of yourself, Mr Parker, you'll be killing yourself one o' these days,' and then she lumbered out into the yard and pushed the baby down the hill.

3

When she came up the hill on the following afternoon it was with the thought of Parker, rather than the hat, uppermost in her mind. She did not conceive the hat as an important thing. Spring was coming across the valley and puffs of blossom, like tranquil smoke, rose everywhere about the pastures below the hill. Under a sharp blue sky the beeches were brilliant masses of almost transparent lace-like leaf and it puzzled her, almost irked her, that a man could live as Parker lived in the spring time: womanless, unswept, curtains unwashed, the old crust of winter still clinging everywhere like a frowsy mould.

So she was glad to see Parker waiting for her by the gate; she was glad to see him looking in so many ways different from the day before. His face was clean and its drunken greyness had gone; he was no longer wearing his best black hat. He was a little working farmer in shirt sleeves, still too narrow of face, too pin-eyed and too cautious, but human and aware.

'How d'you feel to-day, Mr Parker?'

'Ain't so bad.'

'Was your car hurt?'

'It's all right.'

'I said I'd give you bit of a clean-up but I got to git back by four,' she said. 'How if I came in for hour after tea? I could come up.'

'You pick my hat up yesterday?' he said.

'Yes, Mr Parker,' she said. 'I picked it up. I put it in the kitchen.'

'Oh,' he said.

'You never lost nothing, did you?' she said.

'Not as I know on,' Parker said.

She stood by the pram, rocking the baby up and down, talking a little more, and after a time Parker watched her go back through the wood. When she came back soon after six o'clock, without the baby, Parker was not there. She could hear the sound of a tractor down the hill.

The evening was very warm and soft and a deep fragrance of bluebells came from hazel copses above the house as she turned the kitchen furniture into the farmyard and then took the curtains from the windows and hung them, like disintegrating cobwebs, on the clothes line. She scrubbed the kitchen floor, the stove, and the stone steps outside. Water ran like mud, bearing away with it the stale rank odours of old grease, old cooking, old dust, and the curious close stench of winter decay. She washed up the crockery of the past week and opened the windows and let in the spring evening air.

When she had finished all this she walked into the yard to look for Parker. When she could not see him she walked across to a small orchard beyond the cow-barn. Down the hill Parker was harrowing ground for spring seed. The soil was dry and dusty and the tractor seemed to draw behind it a brown and smoky cloud.

Everywhere primroses, with drifts of white anemone, were growing in lush masses under hazel-trees and she gathered a handful while she waited for Parker to come in with the harrow. But after a time there seemed to be something wrong with the tractor and she gave up waiting and went back into the house.

She put the primroses into a little red glass jug on the supper table. She had already laid out all the food she could find, a little bread, a piece of home-killed bacon, and a lump of cheese. Now she sat down to wait for Parker and after about ten minutes he came in.

For some moments he stood on the kitchen threshold with small rabbity eyes transfixed by all he saw. This transfixed narrow stare was not surprised or unbelieving or even doubtful. It was held in suspicion: as if he could not accept it without also accepting that behind it there lay some sort of motive. Nobody did such things for nothing; nobody gave things away without wanting something back.

'I didn't have much time, Mr Parker,' she said, 'but it's a bit better. It's a bit sweeter anyway.'

'Ah,' he said.

'I don't know what you want for supper,' she said. 'That's all I could forage. I'll make you a cuppa tea.'

While she was in the scullery making tea Parker sat at the table in concentration on the food, gnawing with slow greed at lumps of bread.

'You want some new curtains,' she said. 'Them others'll fall to pieces if you wash 'em.'

'I got no money for curtains.'

'Well, it's your place,' she said. 'You wanta look after it.'

'I ain't made o' money,' he said. 'I got a living to git.'

For a second or two it occurred to her to say something about the money in the hat; thirty or forty pounds of it, something that seemed extraordinarily vast to her. It seemed not only incredible but also idiotic that anyone with so much money tucked into the brim of his hat could speak as narrowly and meanly as Parker did. Such dreams as lay in the brim of Parker's hat were stupendous. They were dreams she had often thought about and had never attained.

She said simply instead: 'I'll just pour myself a cup and then run along or else somebody'll be in a two-and-eight at home.'

He drew lumps of pork gristle from his mouth and dropped them on the new-scrubbed floor.

'What's your name?' he said.

'Gaskain.'

'One o' Jim Gaskain's lot?'

'Yes.'

'Which one are you?'

'Dulcima,' she said.

For the first time he smiled. This smile seemed no more than a bristling of dirty teeth from between thin greasy lips, but she was wholly aware of it. It seemed to humanize Parker a little further.

'Funny name, ain't it?' Parker said. 'What do they call you?'

'Dulcie,' she said. 'Or else Dulce.'

'Worse 'n Dulcima,' he said.

She did not answer. She had been a little sorry for Parker; she had been a little puzzled and baffled by him; and now she was hurt. It seemed a poor return for her kindness, and deep down in her there was kindled, for the first time, out of that terse and narrow uncharitableness about her name, a remote spark of resentment.

'Well, I'll be going now,' she said.

He guzzled tea. She waited at the door for a word of acknowledgement, of thanks, of simple recognition for the things she had done, but he did not speak and she said:

'How about them curtains? I could git the stuff for you if you wanted.'

'I'll atta see,'

'Everybody says they're goin' up again,' she said. 'You could save a bit now.'

'Ah?'

'You could save ten or twelve shillings,' she said. 'Very like more. You could be twelve or thirteen shillings in pocket.'

'Ah?' he said. He appeared to consider this possibility; it seemed to appeal to him. Then the sudden touch of humanity that made her feel inexplicably sorry for him came out again:

'Ain't had no new curtains since the missus died.'

'Then it's time you had some,' she said. 'You let me git 'em and fix 'em up.'

He hesitated for some moments longer, and then:

'All right,' he said. 'You git 'em.'

He spoke flatly, staring at the primroses, as if seeing them for the first time.

'I shall want some money,' she said.

'All right,' he said. 'I'll atta see about that.'

*

After that she began to go up to the farm every evening. With the money Parker gave her she bought the material for the curtains and made them and hung them up. They were of bright yellow material, with scrolling scarlet roses, and they flapped like signal flags against the windows of the square drab house on the hill. As summer came on she cleaned through the sitting-room, the stairs and the landing, and then into the three bedrooms above. Parker had slept in a small back bedroom on an iron bedstead, throwing an old army overcoat over himself for extra warmth in winter. She turned him out of this frowsy unwashed room into another and then out of that into another, until the three were cleaned. She beat the dust from the carpets in the farmyard and washed the sheets until they too looked like long rows of signal flags strung out under the summer apple-trees.

From time to time Parker said 'I shall atta settle for your time,' or 'Soon as I git that hayin' done I'll settle up wi' you,' but on all these occasions she would simply look at him with her slow dark eyes, as if searching for something beyond him, and say:

'It don't matter. There's no hurry, Mr Parker. There's plenty of time.'

Summer was dry and beautiful on the hill and in the evenings, from that high point about the farm, the sun seemed to go down very slowly across the plain of deep flat country below. Because of this she got into the habit of waiting for Parker to come in from the fields, no matter how late it was. Now that the rooms were all turned out and tidy it was easier to keep everything clean and sometimes there was nothing to do but lay the table for supper.

While she waited she got into the habit of sitting at the

kitchen table and writing down, in a small black notebook, a little account of all the things she had done. She wrote very simply. She wrote down: 'Mr Parker, April 24th, 1½ hrs, 2/3; Mr Parker, curtain pins and tape, 7/6; Mr Parker, June 8, 2½ hrs, 3/9; Mr Parker, soap and scrubbing brush, 3/6; Mr Parker, making curtains, 16/6.' At the bottom of each page she added up the figure and carried it over to the next. Sometimes she checked it over for a mistake and when she heard Parker coming in from the fields she stuffed the book down between the front of her body and her dress. In that way it made no difference to the solid stoutness of her figure, squabby and shapeless from her bust down to the heavy plodding legs still covered with cotton stockings.

Every Tuesday and Friday Parker came home from market, driving wildly up the hill. She grew so used to it that after a time she got into the habit of going up to the farm a little earlier on those days so that she could take off his shoes where he had fallen on the kitchen floor, and loosen his collar and find his hat. There was always money in the hat, twenty or thirty pounds, and once, after some heifer calves had been sold, fifty or sixty; but she did not touch it. It was as if she did not regard the debt that Parker owed her as having any bearing on this; as if something in Parker or something in herself, his meanness and her own patience, were quite separate, and as if she could wait for a long time, perhaps years, before they came together.

By July summer began to burn the thin earth of the hill-side until the chalk was like dry white flame and there was an evening in late July when she found it too hot to sit in the kitchen. Instead she sat on the stone steps outside, writing her accounts in the small black book, her cotton stockings rolled down, for coolness, over her ankles.

That evening Parker came unexpectedly from the barn behind the house, surprising her. She was torn for a moment between the necessity of hiding the book and the necessity of rolling up her stockings, and she decided on the book. Some moments later Parker was crossing the threshold, stepping over her thick bare legs as he went into the house for supper.

'Everything's on the table,' she said. 'I'll be there in a minute.'

She stretched out her big fleshy legs and began to roll up her stockings and Parker, at the kitchen table, sat watching her.

He watched her for some time longer, across the table, as he ate his meal. Heat came in pulsating thick waves as it rose from the valley. Once again she began to long for a breath of air and suddenly she decided, a little earlier than usual, to get up and go.

As she reached the doorway Parker got up from the table, his eyes curiously excited, and said:

'How about you coming up here for good?' he said. 'I bin wanting to ask you.'

'Me?' she said. 'No.'

'Ah, come on,' he said. 'You like it up here. Don't you like it?'

'I like it.'

'You come up and keep house for me. I'll pay. When you finished in the house you can give me a hand outside. I'll pay.'

'I couldn't,' she said.

'I'll pay.'

'I couldn't.'

'Why?' he said. 'Why? I git on well with you. I'll pay.'

'Oh! I don't know,' she said. It was as if she seemed to give way a little, to consider it. She looked past him with black slow eyes, in remote calculation. 'You keep saying pay but how do I know? What'll you pay?'

'Two pound,' he said. 'And keep.' It was like speaking of an animal. 'Two pound a week.'

'I could get that down in the village. Without traipsing all this naughty way up here.'

She lied flatly, calmly, as if for some time she had prepared herself for it.

'All right. Two pounds ten.'

'Then there's what you owe me.'

'I know, I know that,' he said. Clumsily he tried to grasp

her shoulders but she held herself back, pressed against the doorpost. 'I bin meaning – you didn't think I wadn't goin' to pay, Dulcie, did you? Eh? You didn't think –'

'You'll pay,' she said. 'I know.'

'You come then,' he said, 'will you? Eh? It'll be all right? Two pound ten, eh?'

'I got to think it over. There's –'

'What?' he said. 'There's what?'

'There's a lot of things. Well, there's other people –'

'Ah,' he said. He could not guess now at what she was thinking; she simply gave the impression of holding something back.

'I'll tell you to-morrow,' she said.

When she came back, next day, in the early evening, she was surprised to find him already home from the fields. He had changed his shirt and had put on a clean celluloid collar, high and rather old-fashioned, with a brown clip-on tie.

'You think about what I said?' he asked her.

'A bit.'

'You'll come then, will you? Eh?'

She did not answer; for some time she walked about the kitchen, and then into the scullery and back again, getting his tea. He began to follow her, dog-like, his face in its scrubbed cleanness queerly earnest above the high choking collar.

'It ain't bad up here, is it? You like it, don't you?'

'Yes, but what am I going to do with myself all day? Nobody to talk to – nobody up here.'

'I'll take you into town – market days, Saturdays – no need to be lonely –'

'It ain't that.'

She seemed to dispose of one objection and then suddenly, flatly, emotionlessly, bring up another.

'It ain't only what I think,' she said.

'Who else then? Your dad?'

'No,' she said. 'I don't care about him.'

'Who else then?'

'Well – there's somebody.'

'Who?' he said. 'Who?'

'My boy. My young man.'

'Never knowed you had one.'

'You don't know everything, do you?' she said.

He sat at the table, not answering, confused and very
quiet. He stared down at her strong thick legs and then up
at her arms. The flesh of her arms, for all its plumpness, was
fine and smooth and now in high summer it gleamed a
strong soft brown from sun.

'Don't think he'd want you to?' he said.

'Well, I got to think about him, haven't I?' she said. 'I
got to consider him.'

'What's his name?'

'Albert.'

She spoke readily, lying again about the name as she had
already lied about the young man himself and as yesterday
she had lied about the village and the money. It was as if
she wanted to fire in Parker a terrible and foolish eagerness;
and then in turn to break down, by a series of little things,
the caution in him that had once conceived her as a
trap.

'You think he wouldn't like it?' he said.

'It ain't only that.'

'What else is it?'

She lied again: 'He gives me a few shillings a week,' she
said. 'Saving money. So we can git a few things ready. So
we can be married some day.'

'Married?' he said. The eagerness in him, already roused,
seemed to split his eyes with small fires of helpless bewilder-
ment. 'You goin' git married?'

'Well, some day I hope.'

'Three pound a week,' he said. 'If I give you that, will
you come?'

Once again she looked beyond him with her small dark
eyes.

'I'll ask Albert to-night,' she said. 'He'll probably
murder me.'

4

When she moved in, two days later, with all her belongings packed in a cheap brown fibre suit-case, she gave Parker the impression not that it was something she had long prepared but that it was something she was doing with his own peculiar caution, as a favour, reluctantly.

'I'll try it for a week,' she said. 'I'll give it a trial.'

She moved into the front bedroom and at night she locked her door. She made a point, during those first few days, of speaking often of Albert. She wondered what Albert would say if he could see her now; she wondered what on earth she would do if Albert popped in. Albert came gradually forward into the situation not simply as a third party but as a watchful and terrifying eye, keeping guard on her. She brought him along as a person of possessive and jealous desire. Albert was a terror for getting to know everything; you couldn't keep anything from Albert. Whatever she did Albert got to know. Albert would brain her if she didn't do this and didn't do that. There was no fooling Albert.

On the following Tuesday she and Parker drove down to market together for the first time.

'I only hope we don't see Albert,' she said. 'I had to kid him with all sorts of tales about you.'

Parker felt pleased at this. In his ignorance of her lying he was flattered.

'Never mind about Albert. You keep along o' me,' he said. 'I got a few fly deals on to-day.'

Throughout the day Parker went about the market like a nosing fox. She had grown used to the fact that, up at the farm, he sometimes did not speak much. Now he hardly spoke at all. Now whatever he was thinking seemed to become locked up. The dumb grey eyes flickered occasionally in a tight-drawn face that otherwise had no expression. He leaned on cow-stalls, making bargains, staring at dung-splashed concrete, eyes downcast. She saw him for the first time as a person of ruthless and one-track brain, scheming and cunning, lying too, fanatically pursuing one end. And gradually, beside him, her own thoughts and her own lying seemed very little, quite innocent, of no serious account at all.

During most of that time he did not notice her. Somewhere about noon he went into the *Market Arms* to start the first drinking of the day. She went away alone and bought herself a dinner of roast beef and potatoes and apple tart and afterwards a cup of tea in a back-street dining-rooms. While she drank the tea she wrote in her little book: 'Dinner. July 15. 3/4.'

After that, about two o'clock, she went back to find Parker. She found him drinking, but not drunk; and she pulled nervously at his sleeve:

'Mr Parker, I just seen Albert. I don't know whether he seen me or not but I'm scared of what he'll do.'

'We'd better git home.'

'That's what I thought,' she said.

And once again Parker, because of what she said about Albert, was pleased. It flattered him greatly to think that she was afraid of Albert for his sake. He drove home with a smile on his face and a little more caution than usual: a good day, a hat full of money and now, on top of it, they were kidding Albert. They were running away from Albert together.

In this way they lived for three or four weeks, through July and into harvest. On the hill the summer had been very hot, almost rainless, scorching the barley straw so that it was short, no higher than white grass, and easy to gather. Besides herself Parker had no help except a part-time hand, an oldish man named Barnes, and the three of them worked at the small harvest together.

One afternoon Barnes stopped working and stood staring down the hillside; then he walked forward across the stubble a yard or two and squinted.

'Somebody a-prowlin' about down there,' he said. 'Somebody with a gun.'

'Oh!' she said.

'Where's that?' Parker said.

'Down aside the bottom gate,' Barnes said. 'Young chap. I can see the gun.'

'It looks like Albert,' she said.

After a time the young man with the gun disappeared, and once again Parker got the feeling that he had done very well for himself. Not merely was she a good girl, a willing girl, a hard-working girl; she was a girl that someone else wanted. The thought of Albert jealous, Albert prowling about with a gun, Albert watching her, was something that puffed him with satisfaction.

That evening she was changing in her room when Parker went past on the landing. Her door was open a little. She had taken off her dress and she was stooping over her attaché case, which lay open on the bed.

Parker opened the door slightly and looked in. 'Was wondering where you were,' he said.

'I'm just changing,' she said.

He saw the attaché case open on the bed.

'Ain't goin' nowheres, are you?' he said.

'Oh! I don't know,' she said. 'I don't know. I get worried.'

'Worried?' he said. He came into the bedroom. 'Here, what's this?'

'Well, it's Albert,' she said. 'It's Albert.' She began quickly brushing her hair as if she were nervous, almost a little distracted. 'When people start prowling about with guns I think it's time I got back home – '

'No,' he said. 'Don't do that.'

He came over to her and put his arms across her bare shoulders, clumsily. He began to seem a little distracted too, troubled by the thought of losing her.

'God, no,' he said. 'Don't do that, Dulcie, you can't do that.'

'I can if Albert says so.'

She gave her hair a long deep casual stroke with the brush. That summer, for the first time in her life, she had found time to spend on her hair, and now it brushed out into a thick black fringe that fell over his hands. As she tossed it back again, the dark hair falling over her white plump shoulder, her big breast was strained upward. In a tortured and clumsy way he struggled for a few moments to thrust himself nearer her body, and she pushed him away.

'Here, steady, we're not married.'

'I don't want you to go – '

'Yes, but people prowling about with guns. Besides,' she said suddenly, 'you ain't paid me – '

'I know. I'll pay,' he said. 'I'll pay.'

'You keep saying that.'

'I'll pay,' he said. 'I'll pay to-night. I'll git it after supper.'

'All of it?'

'Yeh,' he said. 'Yeh. All on it. I'll pay.'

'All right,' she said. 'You git it after supper. I'll reckon how much it is.'

She brushed her hair once again with long, casual, and now almost contemptuous swinging of the brush; she brought it down in a black arch over her sun-brown face, tossed it away again, bringing up the arch of her plump white shoulder.

'Don't look so miserable,' she said. 'I ain't gone yet.'

'Don't go,' he said. 'I wouldn't want you to go.'

After supper he got up from the table, looking round with troubled rabbity eyes.

'You want me to pay you now?'

'I could do with it,' she said.

'How much d'ye reckon it'll be?'

'I don't know exactly. I got it all down somewheres,' she said, 'in my room. You git the money. I'll be up there. It ain't so much.'

She spoke casually, off-hand, as if now, after all, the money did not matter. She looked at his furtive face and she saw that he was past being troubled and was almost frightened. Then she recalled his face as she had seen it in the market, making his deals, unrelaxed and relentless, the face of a dumb fox, and it almost surprised her to see now, at last, how excruciating the change in him was.

She went up to her room. She did not look at the little book. Instead she lay full length on the bed, listening, looking at the blue August evening sky, turning the figure in the book over and over in her mind: twenty-one pounds five-and-six, twenty-one pounds five-and-six, twenty-one –

All this time she could hear Parker lumbering in the attic above her head. She had never been up to the attic. A little flight of wooden steps led up to it and the door was always locked. What was up there she did not know but she felt that perhaps soon, now, there would be ways of knowing. She could persuade Parker, perhaps, to tell her what was there. Twenty-one pounds – did it matter what was in the little book? Did it matter to a pound, one way or another? Twenty-four pounds, twenty-seven? Need Parker know? She stared dreaming at the August sky, still quivering with the heat of the day, and decided that Parker need never know.

When at last he came down from the attic and she heard him shuffling in the corridor outside she called:

'You can come in. I found out what it was.'

She turned her face in the bed and looked at him.

'Gettin' lazy, aren't I?'

She gave a long deep sigh, as if against the heat and tiredness of the day, and spread out her plump bare arms across the bed. He stood looking at her for some moments, attracted and bewildered, tortured between the visual image of her lying there, of the dark-haired supine body relaxed as if waiting for him, and the hard and painfully difficult thought that now he must pay her what he owed.

Suddenly all his tortured thought seemed to resolve itself. He came forward another pace or two and began to make trembling and clumsy efforts to touch her.

'Here,' she said, 'this won't get the money paid –'

Once again he was human and tender.

'I want you,' he said. His hands were beginning to tremble violently. 'I want you – I can't git on without you –'

'You keep all on, don't you? Mind my dress.'

'Dulcie,' he said. 'God –'

'Mind my dress then. And don't call me Dulcie. My name's Dulcima.'

'Dulcima,' he said quietly. 'Dulcima.'

He ran his hands about her relaxed soft throat and shoulders, trembling, seeking with gestures of great clumsiness to express what he felt and what he wanted.

'Here, I thought you came to pay me the money,' she said.

'I did. So I did. I got it.'

'Put it on the wash-stand then,' she said. He seemed to hesitate. 'Go on –'

She lingered on the words and something about them seemed to inflame him, so that he moved almost blindly as he groped about, taking the money from his trousers' pocket. 'How much?' he said. 'How much?'

'Forty pounds,' she said. 'Just forty. Well, all but two shilling –'

For a moment he was shattered. He had moved across to the wash-stand like a man in a coma of heavy excitement and now, for a single moment, the notion of that extraordinary figure of forty pounds seemed to wake him up. He turned on her sharply. His mouth gaped open as if, in a flash of revelation, he had seen what a fool he was.

And then he stopped. He saw that she had taken off her dress and that now she was sitting up on the bed, casually and half undressed, rolling down her stockings. He heard her say something about 'put it in the drawer, it'll be out of the way there' and in blind excitement he stuffed what money he had into the drawer of the wash-stand.

When he groped back to her it was to be stricken by another troubling and this time more painful thought.

'What about Albert?' he said.

'You don't think I ever wanted Albert,' she said, 'do you?'

She looked past him with a long slow smile.

'Did Albert ever –?'

'Does it matter if he did?' she said.

Frenziedly he reached out for her and she smiled, letting him kiss her for the first time. She held her face sideways, so that the black close eyes were fixed on the evening sky. The evening was still warm and blue and beautiful and now she seemed to see something in it that split the dark pupils for another second with yet another smile.

5

She did not go to market on the following day. 'I'll glean a little corn for the hens,' she said. 'You enjoy yourself. You'll get on better without me.'

During the morning, when Parker had gone, she discovered, for the first time, what lay in the little attic above the steps and what, in turn, lay above that too.

Parker, the previous night, had left his working clothes in her bedroom. In the morning she had taken the key of the attic from his trousers and later he had gone away in the suit, with the black hat, he always wore for market.

When she went up into the little attic she was surprised to find it empty except for a shelf on which stood rows of biscuit tins. At first she did not bother to look into these tins. She went up another flight of steps on to the roof above. A square balustraded platform had been built there by some previous owner who had evidently wanted the air, the stars, the sun or simply the long view, across twenty miles of valley, to the sea.

She stood for some time fascinated by this view. It opened out a world that lay below her like a map. She could see not only the fields she knew, bare and white after the heat of summer and harvest, but small chalky veins of road winding away among clotted copses of sweet chestnut, through fox-red villages and fields of dark green potatoes. She could see, five or six miles away, the square stone church tower of the market town and then, far beyond it, delicate and faint, the line of sea horizon, with a few creeping charcoal puffs that were the smoke of passing steamers. It created for her the curious and heady illusion that here, above everything, alone and on top of the world, she had never been able to see so far.

After some minutes she went down into the attic. She smiled occasionally when she thought of Parker: Parker so clever, so tight, so mean and so eager; Parker so desperate for her, so childish and so like a man. She smiled when she thought of his rushing, clumsy affection and she smiled still more when she opened the first of the biscuit tins.

In them, in many neat tied bundles of notes, Parker kept his money. There were six biscuit tins and there were even empty biscuit tins waiting to be filled.

At first she did not touch the money. Instead she went back to her bedroom. She found the money Parker had given her and she counted it. There were fifteen pounds.

As she discovered it, she smiled another curious sideways smile and then went back to the attic. She opened one of the biscuit tins and took another twenty-five pounds; and then, as an afterthought, another ten. Then she closed the biscuit tins and went downstairs.

All that day she did as she had told Parker she would: she gleaned corn for the hens from the lower wheat field. It was very hot in the white chalk cup of land below the hill and she felt the sun burn her as she worked solidly up and down with heavy movements of her thick brown legs and arms. Work and the long hot summer had taken a little flesh from her, so that her limbs were harder and smoother, without the flabbiness of the days when she had pushed the pram up the hill. Her dark eyes were keener and brighter, more penetrating and more mature. She had found more time to brush her hair and gradually it had lost its coarseness. She even thought there were times when her legs were not so ugly as before.

Once during the afternoon she looked up and there, at the foot of the hill, by the gate, she saw once again the young man with the gun, the man that Barnes had seen. He seemed to hesitate for a moment as she looked up, and then he began to walk across the field towards her.

She went on gathering corn-straw until he came up to

her. He was very much taller than she was, with a big frame
and a shock of thick fair hair that pushed from under his
cap.

'Beg pardon, Mrs Parker.'

'Who are you calling Mrs Parker?'

'Oh,' he said. In this awkward moment he could do
nothing but look away from her, fidgeting with the stock of
his gun. 'Well – I only wanted to say – I got young pheasants
up in the wood there. Sometimes they get across here on
your piece –'

'If they get on here they belong here,' she said.

'Yes, but –'

'He don't like people roaming about the land. Parker
don't like it, pheasants or no pheasants.'

'I only want to walk across once in a while,' he said. 'Say
once a day.'

'I think you better keep off,' she said. 'He don't like it.'

'Not if I asked him?'

'Wouldn't make no difference. He don't like folks
traipsing round.'

'Would you ask him?'

'Me?'

'I'd be glad if you'd ask him,' he said, 'will you?'

'Well, I'll see,' she said. 'But for the lord's sake don't
come on until I say. He's funny that way. He don't like
people on here.'

'I see. Well, thanks,' he said and began to walk away.

Twenty yards away something seemed to occur to him
and he turned and called back:

'If you want me any time I'm up in the wood. I got a hut
there. You'll find me.'

When Parker came home about four o'clock he was less
drunk than sleepy. 'Let me take your hat and coat,' she
said. 'You have a nap in the chair.'

She took his hat and coat and laid them in the sitting-
room. After a time she looked into the hat. Sixty-five
pounds, all in notes, were folded into the brim, and she took
out fifteen. She laid the fifteen pounds on the kitchen table

and when Parker woke up and came to the table for tea she said:

'This is that money you give me last night. I did say fourteen, didn't I?'

'Yeh, yeh,' he said. He spoke with sleepy eagerness; he remembered how, the previous night, she had clearly spoken of forty and of how he had put only fifteen, in that tense excited moment of seeing her undressing, in the wash-stand drawer. 'Yeh, that was it, fourteen.'

'Well you give me too much. You give me fifteen.'

'I did?'

'You better have a pound back,' she said. 'We want things right, don't we?'

'No, no, go on,' he said. 'That's for you. You have it. You keep that.' He smiled and leaned across the table and ran his hand briefly about her neck. 'That's for you. That's for the little extras.'

She smiled too, sleepy and casual, and said, letting him caress her: 'You like the little extras, do you?'

He was fired with small frenzies of excitement and leaned farther over and kissed her face, brown and warm from sun. She laughed and suddenly it seemed to him marvellously good and clever and satisfying to have her there, to have got away with the small deceit of the fifteen pounds, and to hear her laughing because he touched her.

'You better get on with your tea,' she said. 'There's a time and place –'

He tried roughly to smother her mouth with kisses and she said:

'Go on with you. You'll knock your tea over and then you'll know about it.'

Then as he laughed and let her go, she said:

'About this money. It's quite a bit. I thought I'd bank it.'

'Banks? You don't want t'ave nothing to do with no banks,' he said. 'Banks ain't no good.'

'No?'

'They git to know too much. They know all your business. Then the income tax git to know. I ain't payin' no tax if I know it – they ain't gittin' nothing away from me.'

'I'll put it in the post office,' she said. 'I'll git interest.'

'You don't wanta do nothing with it,' he said. 'You keep it. You keep it where nobody can't touch it. That's all.'

'Well, I'll see,' she said.

Suddenly, off-hand, casually, as if it were something of no great importance, she changed the subject.

'Oh! I forgot –' She was telling the truth now; there was no need to lie any longer when she could simply repeat the details of a straightforward circumstance – 'that fellow with the gun – he come prowling round again to-day.'

'Albert?'

'I don't know, I don't know,' she said. In sudden nervousness she spoke quickly. 'He was right across the field. He sheered off through the wood before I could tell.'

'I'll sheer him off,' he said. 'Damn quick. 'What's he want with you now?'

'I don't know, I can't think,' she said. 'Why don't he leave us alone. I told him, I told him about –'

'Told him?' he said. 'Told him about what?'

'About us,' she said. 'About how we were. You know – about being on our own up here and all that. The two of us.'

Parker, with thoughts buzzing in his head like crazy flies, trembled with joy. He suddenly exulted in the notion that he had cheated Albert. At first he had simply been jealous of Albert, but now he had cheated him. It was a clever deal to have cheated Albert. It was a wonderful thing to know that Albert had been rejected.

And now, because of it, he felt more sure of Dulcima. Once or twice he had not been quite so sure. Sometimes when she had spoken of Albert it evoked in him the small, sour, disturbing thought that she was not playing straight with him, that it was really always Albert she liked most, Albert she preferred.

But now he knew that that was not so. Things were different now. Albert was finished, and it was only himself she wanted.

6

Two days later she put her money in the post office bank.
She rode down to the town by bus, coming back in the afternoon with the new clean post office book in her handbag,
thinking how pleasant the first figure in it was; how solid
and how satisfactory and how secret; and how, in time, if
she were careful and things went well, she could make this
figure grow.

The bus stopped on the corner below the hill. She had to
walk the last mile to the farm. In two or three days it would
be September. A few late fingers of honeysuckle, pale yellow,
touched with flecks of strawberry, were still flowering on the
high bank above the lane and she suddenly felt an impulse
to climb the bank to gather them.

From there she could see across a copse of hazel that had
been cut down in springtime. Beyond it great beeches, still
green, faintly brown only when scorched by sun, rose for
almost a mile along the steep hillside of chalk. And as she
stood there, gathering the honeysuckle, smelling it, thinking
a little, she saw the young keeper walking down the path.

He saw her at the same moment and began to come
down beside the hazel copse, almost as if he had been waiting
for her. She saw him coming and began to behave at once
as if she had not seen him, going on gathering the honeysuckle, turning her back, slowly walking away down the hill.

'I got something I wanted to say,' he said.

'Oh?'

Slowly she picked off sprigs of honeysuckle, not looking at
him.

'I been wanting to see you,' he said.

'Me? Why me?'

'I wanted to say I was sorry I called you Mrs Parker.'

She did not speak for a moment. She held her head sideways and put the honeysuckle to her nose and the curling
flowers of it seemed to climb, tendrilwise and delicate, about
her brown cheeks. It was like a small gesture of enticement
that she had made unintentionally.

'I'm sorry I said that,' he said. 'I didn't know.'

'Didn't know what?'

'Well –'

'You don't want to get ideas in your head.'

'I only just come here,' he said. 'I don't know folks –'

'Still, you don't want to get ideas,' she said. 'I don't like people getting ideas.'

He stood awkwardly, not knowing what to say. The hedge, with its pale yellow curling fingers of honeysuckle, stood between them like a barrier. Something made her run her fingers through the topmost leaves of it as she turned and moved along it and then he called:

'There was something else. Did you ask him?'

'Ask him what?'

'About the pheasants – about walking over –'

'I told you it's more than my life's worth,' she said. 'He flies into a two-and-eight now if anybody so much as looks at the land.'

'Shall I ask him?' he said.

'You want to get your brains blown out?' she said.

She held the honeysuckle to her face again and once more, fine and tendrilwise, the flowers delicately fingered the skin of her summer-brown face and once more she responded by walking away.

'The honeysuckle's nice,' he said.

'Yes. It smells nice. I like the smell.'

'There's been a fine lot farther along the wood,' he said, 'on top of the hill.'

'Really?'

'It's nice up there,' he said. 'Nobody ever goes much up there.'

Later, as she walked away across the hill, she was aware of him still standing there, still watching her. She was aware also of wanting to look back. She did not look back and she began to feel vaguely uneasy about something without knowing what it was. A light prickling of sunlight came down through the beech-leaves and made a pattern of light and shadow on her face. Unconsciously she let the honeysuckle finger her mouth again, and it made her look more thoughtful than ever.

Some evenings later, when she sat at supper with Parker, she began to cry.

'Here,' Parker said. 'Here. What now?'

'I can't find the money,' she said. 'That money you give me.'

'Musta mislaid it somewheres, that's all.'

'I looked high and low,' she said.

'When'd you see it last?'

'That day I was gleaning,' she said. 'That day Albert was prowling around. I went out and never locked the house.'

'Gawd,' Parker said. 'We gotta stop this.'

'Don't do nothing yet,' she said. 'We don't want no trouble.'

She cried again as Parker looked about him with small uneasy rabbity eyes.

'Don't cry,' he said. 'That won't do no good.'

'Yes, but I got nothing now. What have I got? I paid all that out – them curtains and all that – and now it's gone –'

'I'll make it up to you. I'll make it right,' Parker said.

After some time she stopped crying.

'I made a mistake that first time,' she said. 'I added it up wrong. You put me off that night, coming into the bedroom. It's twenty-four pounds ten to be right. I forgot two stewpans and I never put the curtain-tapes down.'

Parker looked troubled and reflective. Several months had gone by since that first evening she had washed his face and talked of new curtains; and it was hard now, almost impossible, to work out how much he might have owed.

'It's only a bit extra,' she said. 'It's not much.' Now she in turn took his head in her hands and smoothed his face. 'You can't have all the little extras for nothing, can you?'

For some days Parker was troubled about the money. He began to make furtive and inconclusive searches among the biscuit tins. He had never been quite sure, to within forty or fifty or even a hundred pounds, how much they held; some times when he came home from market, over-drunk, jubilant at the thought of fifty or sixty pounds folded into his hat, he had woken up to find himself on the kitchen floor, some part of his memory paralysed, so that he could not remember exactly how much the hat had held.

At the same time his thoughts of Dulcima deepened. He thought of how good she was, how capable, how hardworking; how she had got her head screwed on the right way. He thought much more of her brown, smooth, hardening body; he thought of her as she was in the bedroom. He felt that if he married Dulcima he could take her into his confidence. He would be able to tell her about the money upstairs. He had the impression that she was a shrewd careful girl who perhaps could help him, in time, to make more money. That was the sort of partner he wanted.

Then again, he would think, it was cheaper to marry. Three pounds a week: that was a lot of money for a girl, too much money. The two of them could live for that. They could, he thought, enjoy all that they were enjoying now but enjoy it more often and enjoy it cheaper. Marriage was the thing; marriage was the answer.

Then he remembered too that she had once been going to marry Albert and his jealousy about Albert began to be renewed. It was odd how Albert was always cropping up. He remembered the incident of Albert in the wheatfield, staring over the gate with his gun, Albert at the market, Albert prowling round, Albert having to be told about things, Albert always after her. He remembered how once the notion of Albert doing these things had seemed funny and how he thought he had cheated him. But now it was not funny; he was not so sure. He began to want Dulcima for himself. More and more he wanted to be sure of her and to be rid of Albert for ever.

So he spoke of getting married. 'Eh? How about that?' he said. 'You know how folks are – start talkin'. We could git married at one o' them offices any day. Eh?'

'I got to think it over.'

'All right, you think it over.'

And as the days passed she would think it over; or rather

she would pretend to think it over. She would think instead of her bank-book, the money in the biscuit tins, and the way the money could grow; she would smile at the thought of Parker and his little extras and how, for some time longer, she would keep him waiting for an answer.

Then as the days grew shorter, Parker began to think of long winter nights, with western winds howling wet sea-storms against the hill. He thought of snow. Sometimes snow lay so long and deep in the narrow hill-lanes that he could not get out for a month to the market. He felt he did not want to face the snow, the storms, the darkness, and the rain alone again in another winter. He dreaded a cold empty bed and the dark crust of winter settling over everything as it had done last year, before Dulcima had arrived to sweep it away.

'Well, Dulcie, you made up your mind –?'

'Oh! I don't know. I want to – it ain't that, but there's a lot o' things –'

'It ain't Albert, is it?'

'Albert – good Lord, no.'

'What is it then?'

'Well, once you're married, you're married. I don't want to jump out of the frying pan into the fire,' she said, laughing, 'do I?'

'When are you going to make up your mind? Soon, eh? Afore winter?'

'Some day.'

She noticed how her little trick of mocking him started fires of excitement in his eyes. 'Course you might have to marry me, yet. You know that, don't you?'

'That wouldn't worry me,' he said.

'I should think not,' she said, 'I'm the one to worry about a thing like that.'

'You think it over then – quick,' he said. 'Think it over – afore winter comes.'

But as she lay awake at night, on the soft windless dark-ness of early October, she did not think it over. She thought of other things. She thought mostly, at first, of the money, the biscuit tins, the bank-book and the simple way she had been able to arrange these things. She thought of how easily, after all, she had been able to get the things she had never had. She remembered her father, the barrier standing between herself and a new dress or new shoes or new white gloves or a little freedom or a little money. She remembered the children coming one after another, and then the days with the pram, all of them frustrating her. Now she was finished with them all: the children, her father, the pram, the days of tugging and standing and pushing until her legs were gross and hideous, and she was glad that they were over.

She thought also of the young man standing by the hedge of honeysuckle, watching her as she walked away through the wood of beeches. She remembered the curious sensation that seemed to impel her to turn round and look back at him. In the warm October darkness it was a sensation that somehow began to magnify itself. It grew not only larger but more mystifying. It fascinated and haunted her, so that she lay awake for a long time with her eyes stiffened with sleeplessness, staring at the stars above the hill, wondering why it fascinated her and why it roamed tirelessly and hauntingly round and round in her mind.

Then, at last, it began to trouble her.

7

One afternoon in late October she walked through the beech-wood, above the farm, to the keepers' hut on the far slope of the hill. The leaves of the beeches were already making masses of fire against a sky that was blue and lofty and under them the glow of air was a pure orange, full of dancing flies.

The door of the keepers' hut was open but the hut was empty and her feeling of disappointment was so sharp that it took her by surprise. She had not expected that. Inside the hut there was a table, a camp-bed, two chairs, an oil-stove and a few cups and a box below the bed. A row of oiled steel traps hung on one wall and a neat pile of newspapers lay on the table, with a pair of leather gloves and a canvas bag.

She felt a curious uneasy sensation of excitement as she looked at these things. There was a neatness, a swept home-liness about the hut that fascinated her. A bucket with a galvanized lip for soap stood in one corner with a towel folded over the side. A mirror by the window above it had a hairbrush and comb hanging on one side and a razor-strop on the other.

For winter there was a stove and for some reason she thought suddenly of winter rain, of days of flying beech-leaves, of the little hut with the stove humming away behind the closed door. There was something wonderfully secure in thinking about these things, and that too took her by surprise.

She walked away up the hill. At the crest of it a breeze came over the bare western slope where the copses of hazel had been cut down. It blew her hair about her face and down over her cheeks in untidy strands. The honeysuckle the young man had spoken about had dropped its flowers and now hung with reddening berries over bushes of haw-thorn.

She walked back down the hill. Half-way to the hut the sound of a gun-shot came from the far side of the wood, rushing like a rocket through the fiery ceiling of leaves. She went on and stood for some moments at the door of the hut. This time she noticed on the wall inside a pattern of blown birds' eggs, some hundreds of them, blue and white and scribbled and spotted and brown, strung together in neck-laces, the eggs graded like beads. They too fascinated her. They too had that wonderful neatness and secureness about them that left her uneasy and surprised.

As she went inside the hut to look more closely at the pattern of eggs making ten-fold necklaces on the dark wall, she caught sight of her face with its untidy strands of blown hair in the mirror by the window.

She stood by the mirror and began to comb back her hair with her fingers. Her hair had always tended to grow in heavy side-fingers that had the effect of thickening her face. It grew low over her forehead and was greasy. Suddenly she picked up the comb and began to comb the wind-blown strands of hair back from her forehead and her ears. The sensation of the comb scraping over the crest of her forehead and through her matted hair was so minutely painful for a moment that she bit her lips. She was angry with herself and suddenly hated the face she saw in the mirror, with the too thick, too dark, too greasy hair. It brought back for a moment a memory of her father. She felt a stab of her old grievance about being beautiful. She remembered how much she had wanted to have a different body: a different kind of face, different eyes, different hands, above all different legs and hair.

'Who would look at a face like that?' she thought.

She was savagely brushing her hair when she heard the young man set his gun down by the door of the hut. She was so startled that she had no time to put down the brush. She felt the blood rushing to her face and then an embarrassing trembling of her hands.

'It's all right. Make yourself at home,' he said. 'I saw you coming down.'

'You saw me?'

'Not many people I miss,' he said. 'That's what I'm here for.'

'I didn't think you saw me –'

She did not know what to do with the brush in her hands.

'I'm using your brush – the wind got into my hair. I can never do anything with it. I don't know what you'll think of me –'

'That's all right,' he said.

'I really come in to look at your birds' eggs. The door was open and I could see them and I come in.'

'That's all right.'

The blood was pounding up through her neck and face and into the roots of her hair, and she was gripping the brush with both hands.

'I'm sorry – it's not very nice coming in like that and using other people's brushes and all that – but I never thought –'

'I'm going to make some tea,' he said. 'What about a cup o' tea?'

'I think I ought to go,' she said. 'I think I made a nuisance of myself enough for one day.'

'That's all right. Stay and have a cup o' tea.'

She watched him, still with the brush in her hands, put a match to a little oil stove on a stand by the window. She saw him fill an enamel kettle from a bucket underneath it. He put two mugs on the table, with a tin of sugar and a bottle of milk, and a teapot and two spoons. She was fascinated again by the neatness of everything, the order, the completeness of his private world.

'You always live here?' she said.

'March to November.'

'You sleep here?'

'Everything,' he said.

He turned to find a chair for her and she saw his eyes shine pale blue, almost white, in the brilliance of low October light by the doorway.

'Don't you find it lonely?'

'Me? No: I like it.'

'I think I should find it lonely.'

'Depends what you're used to,' he said.

It was only when she turned to sit down at last that she became aware again of the brush. She was still trembling as she laid it on the little shelf under the mirror.

'I don't know what you think of me – with your brush and all that –'

But he was pouring water into the teapot, with his back to her, and did not answer.

In her nervousness, as she sat at the table with him, drinking tea, she could think of nothing to talk about but the long necklaces of blown eggs hanging behind him on the wall. The semi-circles of blue and brown and white framed his face each time she turned to look at him.

'Them?' he said. 'That's my score. Three hundred and twenty since March.'

'That keeps you busy. That's why you're not lonely,' she said.

'Found a magpie's only last week,' he said. 'It's one I missed somehow: one egg.'

'That was one for sorrow,' she said. 'Or is it joy? I can never remember.'

'I don't know. They're all magpies to me. All vermin. I can't bother about sorrow or joy.'

And then: 'Talking about my score, I think the brush makes us even. You know – for when I called you Mrs Parker.'

'Oh! that.'

All of a sudden she was astonished by a wave of repugnance about Parker. It rushed up into her head to chill the last of the hot blood of her embarrassment about the brush.

'I didn't think,' he said. 'You know – it was natural.'

'I just housekeep for him,' she said. 'He got nobody to look after him after his wife died. I felt sorry for him. I just did it to oblige. That's all – I shan't stay long.'

'No?'

'No. I don't want to stay there all my life, do I?'

For some moments he did not speak again. He held the mug of tea just under his face, in both hands, his elbows on the table, his lips blowing slightly. On his top lip the hairs were long and soft and remarkably golden as if the sun bleached them as they grew freshly every day.

'Do you sleep there?' he said.

'Who me?' she said. 'Not likely. I go back home every night.'

As she lied she felt a rush of new embarrassment spring up and meet, in a sickening impact, the cold wave of a new repugnance about Parker.

'Here, I hope you don't get ideas,' she said. 'I hope you don't think –'

'No,' he said. 'No. I didn't mean –'

'I should hope not. I should think so,' she said. 'It's bad

44

enough having to be stuck up here, all alone half the time. Half the time nobody to talk to. Nobody to see –'

'Well, now you can come and see me,' he said.

She felt at that moment a wave of quite different feeling gather and slowly proceed, without violence, up through her body. It had the effect of softening, then dispelling the last of her embarrassment and she said:

'Is that asking me? Is it an invitation?'

'I like somebody to talk to –'

'Is it an invitation?'

'Yes,' he said.

The remarkable flow of new warm feeling spread at last over all her body, making her smile.

'Will you come?'

'Yes,' she said. 'I'd like to.'

Later, as she walked down the path through the wood, away from the hut, she had again the curious feeling that he was watching her from behind. She was harassed by an overwhelming instinct that she must turn and look at him. This time she did turn, and then when she turned he was not there. Only clouds of golden October flies were dancing by the hut in the sunshine.

That night she lay awake for longer than usual. She thought of the incredible private neatness of the hut: the skeins of birds' eggs, the singing of the kettle on the stove, the smell of tea and oil and spent cartridges, the way she had brushed her hair. She remembered his question about where she slept at nights and what she had said in answer.

'I done wrong about that,' she thought. 'I never ought to have said that.' She felt a sudden complication of thought that was too much for her. She stared sleeplessly, in remorse, at the October stars.

'Now I don't know where I am,' she thought. 'I don't know where I am.'

8

As October went on she began to walk up into the wood almost every afternoon. 'I'll see for a few blackberries,' she would say to Parker, 'else a few nuts.' Or she would suddenly get her black leather shopping bag and say, as if on the spur of the moment: 'I just remembered I got no baking powder in the house. I'll walk down as far as the shop. Is there anything you want? I'll bring it if you do.'

Sometimes the door of the hut was open and the hut itself empty. She would stand outside under the gleaming orange October beeches or sit inside at the neat swept table, waiting for a while. She would find herself fascinated again by the neatness of everything, the seclusion, the clean and solid privacy. She would feel herself grow excited by the smell of oil in traps, of tea, of spent cartridges and dying leaves. Then she would suddenly feel sick about Parker. Her repugnance about him would begin to drive her like an ugly rat. She would feel, again, that she did not know where she was. She was lost somewhere between the haunting repugnance about Parker and the haunting nervousness about the keeper, whose name she did not know. And suddenly she would turn and hurry back down the hill, through flying shoals of beech-leaves, frightened of herself, back to Parker and the farm.

On another day the young man would be sitting in the hut, alone and quiet, exactly as she pictured him and exactly as she wanted him to be. She would sit for a time talking, listening to the quiet flame of the stove. He would make tea and she would watch, in stillness, but without assurance or confidence, the movement of his large bony hands.

Then she would try, with hesitation, awkwardly, to find what lay behind the calmness, the assured quietness, the half-averted, pale, transparent eyes.

Didn't he ever go down to market? To the pictures once in a while?

'No,' he said. 'By the time I'm finished and cleaned up here I'm about ready for bed.'

Didn't he feel he wanted an evening out some time? Didn't he feel he'd go off his head up there, alone in the wood, same thing day after day, without a bit of a change?

'I sometimes get down as far as the main road on Sundays,' he said. 'Walk down and watch the cars.'

'You do?' she said. 'I go that way sometimes. Do you know *The Rose of Tralee*? That's down there. On the corner. It's a café.'

'No,' he said. 'I just walk round.'

'They have tea,' she said, 'and ice-cream and all that. You can have it in the garden. They have tables in the garden.'

'That's nice,' he said.

'They wanted me to work there once,' she said. 'In the kitchen. They offered me a good job there once. I sometimes think I should have took it. I sometimes think I ought to go down and ask them if they still wanted anybody. What do you think?'

'You should go down,' he said.

'Yes,' she said, 'I think I'll walk down on Sunday. What time do you go down?'

'Most Sundays I got to be here,' he said. 'If I got a big shoot on Monday I got to get ready for that.'

She noticed he spoke with half-averted eyes, as if he were a long way away from her: as if, she thought, he could not bear to come nearer or even look at her.

One afternoon she did not walk up to the wood. She took the bus and her big black shopping bag and went into town. She had begun to experience a sudden hunger for new shoes. She felt the need for a pair of gloves for her hands. She was troubled once again by the ugliness of her feet and hands and legs, the clumsy shortness of her body. She spent some time in shoe shops, buying herself finally a pair of black patent shoes with oval buckles and then a lighter pair, pale grey, with higher heels, in suede. She had never before had money for shoes like that and suddenly she felt driven by a new excitement.

'And stockings? Would you want stockings?' the assistant said. 'We keep stockings.'

As Dulcima fingered the silk stockings with her coarse and stumpy hands she recalled, once again with hatred, the ugliness of her thick legs and ankles. She bought three pairs of stockings and then 'I gotta get a dress too,' she thought. 'No sense having new shoes and stockings and not a dress.'

For the rest of the afternoon, as she went from shop to shop, it was as if she peeled off old skins of her life: shoes, cotton stockings kept up with black garters, straight print dress bleached by sun and washing, old underwear having broken straps fixed up with safety pins. As she tried on dresses in fitting cubicles she was more and more painfully aware of the shabbiness, the sloppy shapelessness of herself. The dresses seemed like stretched sacks on her big breasts and waist and thighs. 'It's not that you're bad for size,' assistants told her. 'But you need support. You would find it better with support.' She had never bothered with corsets and sometimes, alone up at the farm, in hot weather, with only Parker to see her, not even with a brassière. Now she bought them. She saw herself as she had seen so many advertisements of women, over and over again, in news-papers and magazines: her breasts cupped and held upright, her short thick back and thighs curved in oyster, the stretch-ed front of herself gleaming silkily.

She bought a pair of white kid gloves and she thought finally of a hat. It took her some time to decide against a hat. She decided on a perm for her hair instead. 'You will have to make an appointment,' they told her and she said:

'It has to be before Sunday. I got to have it before Sun-day.'

'We can manage Friday,' they said. 'At three in the afternoon.'

When she got back to the farm after going to the hair-dresser on Friday afternoon Parker had not come home from market. She went upstairs and sat in her bedroom and stared at herself in the glass. She saw her face as she might have seen the face of another person. She felt it was strange and unreal and beautiful. 'You're rather on the short side,' the hairdresser had said, 'so I'm going to build it up a bit to give you height.' Her hair was mounted now in a series of stiff black lustreless waves that, rising to a crown, made her face seem longer and less podgy. The untidy strands that had covered her ears and the sides of her cheeks had been cut away. She was able to see, almost as it might have been for the first time, the shape of her ears. Free of hair, they were surprisingly long and shapely and they too, she thought, had the effect of uplifting her.

For some moments she ran a comb through her hair very gently, hardly daring to touch it. 'Comb it out carefully,' the hairdresser had said. 'It will look better when you have combed it and it has settled down.'

Then she remembered the young man in the wood and suddenly she had an overpowering desire to go up to the keeper's hut and discover what he felt about the strange and lovely change in herself. She did not think he could fail to see, as she did, a transformation.

'I never thought I could look like that,' she thought.

Then she wondered about her clothes. If the change in her hair could do so much for her what about the change in her clothes? She considered for a moment the idea of putting them on and then she thought:

'No. Sunday'll do. I'll wait till Sunday. I'll have a good strip-wash and be clean for Sunday.'

Then suddenly the overpowering desire to show herself to the young keeper came back. She wanted to share the sight of herself, so much changed, with another person.

She gave a final touch or two to her hair with the comb and then went downstairs. It took only a few minutes to go up to the wood, but she wanted to run with excitement. The smell of her hair was something new in her experience too and she wondered if he would notice its strong sweetness. It seemed to her to have a smell that was wonderfully dusky, a deep clove, like the smell of carnations.

In the kitchen Parker was slowly counting money, note by note, out of the greasy rim of his hat. She stopped abruptly. She had forgotten Parker. She was embarrassed and repelled by the sudden realization of Parker. She was sickened by the sight of the greasy hands pawing, with measured greed, into the greasy recesses of the hat.

'Eh, that you, Dulcima? I wondered where you was.'

The bleary eyes of Parker seemed to be pencilled, at the edges, with lines of sharp raw pink. He squinted at her as if he could not see her properly.

A few notes fell out of his unsteady hands into the bowl of his hat and he did not pick them up again. He seemed to grope, with moist, pink-lidded eyes, to focus a better impression of her.

'Dulcie – eh, Dulcie – what you done to yourself? What you bin doing to yourself?' he said.

'I had my hair done, that's all,' she said.

He groped for a moment or two longer in bleary astonishment, trying to correct the focus of the incredible image of her and the unfamiliar mass of piled curled hair.

She did not move. He seemed to be trying to convince himself that what he saw was not a drunk's illusion. He got up and began to come towards her with open hands, the pink-lidded eyes protuberant and inflamed.

'What made you do that?' he said. 'Makes you look different – I like it, it makes you look different. It looks nice. I like it – what made you have it done?'

'I had it done with that money you give me,' she said.

The excited notion flew down through his stupefied brain that, since she had done it with the money he had given her, she had also done it for himself.

'Dulcie, Dulcie,' he said. He began to grope for her neck and shoulders with excited, trembling hands. His nostrils gave a quivering upward start as he caught the extraordinary dusky smell of her hair. 'Dulcie, Dulcie,' he said, 'you thought any more about what I said – you know, about us, about what I said – ?'

'No,' she said. 'No. Not yet – I want to wait a bit – I want to wait.'

She stood rigid while he began to pour wet kisses on her neck and cheeks and soft exposed ears.

'I can't wait much longer,' he said. 'Dulcie, I can't wait much longer –'

'I want to wait,' she said.

'Wait what for?' he said. 'What for? You know me, don't you? You bin here all summer – you know the place, don't you? You know what I got. I got plenty – I got more'n I know what to do with, Dulcie. I bin fly – I got plenty –'

'I want to wait,' she said.

He staggered about the table, reaching for his hat, picking up notes, laughing as he tried to give her the money.

'I got plenty – you only got to say –'

'I don't want it. I want to wait,' she said.

'Here,' he said. 'Here –'

He suddenly seized her by the shoulders, laughing again, dragging her out of the room and upstairs. She let herself be drawn rigidly, without a word. 'You come with me, Dulcie – you come with me. I got summat to show you –' Trying to find his keys, he stumbled, fell on all fours and crawled the last few steps to the attic door on hands and knees.

'There y'are, Dulcie,' he said. 'What about that, eh? You never seen nothing like that afore.'

She stood in the attic staring at the rows of biscuit tins. She had no surprise about them and her hands were stiff by her sides.

'That's money for you, ain't it?' he said.

'I don't want it,' she said.

She found herself staring out of the window, her mind wandering, all her vision expanding out of the narrowness of the little room, out of the world of Parker, the money and the biscuit tins, to the valley lying below in the late October sunshine. In the sharp autumn air its distances seemed to be heightened and enlarged, taking her farther away than ever.

'There y'are,' Parker said. In a stupefied ecstasy of secret-sharing he fingered the money with one hand and then her-self, in clumsy excitement, with the other. 'You don't want no more'n that, do you?'

She stared out of the window into a world whose distances seemed not only amazingly enlarged. They seemed to be pulsating, out as far as the quivering edges of horizon, bluish-copper from approaching sunset, with the deep dis-charge of her own emotions. She thought of the things she had bought herself: the shoes, the silk stockings, the under-wear, the tight sleek corsets, the dress, and even, at last, the pair of white gloves that would hide her big coarse hands. She wanted suddenly to find them all and rush out with them, away from the ugly rat of her repugnance about Par-ker, and never come back.

'I want to wait,' she said.

'All right, you wait,' Parker said. 'Here – take a pound or two now. Buy yourself something nice.' He began to thrust notes into her hands and then, when her hands were too rigid to take them, into the neck of her dress. 'You take 'em – buy something – just for yourself.'

She was hardly aware of what he did to her.

'How long d'ye want to wait?' he said.

'Not long now,' she said. 'Not long.'

9

She lay awake for a long time in the night, thinking again of the clothes she had bought, coming slowly to a decision. She felt she could not wait even another day before she wore them for the first time. She came to a decision, too, about another thing.

'I got to go. I got to get out,' she thought. 'I don't know where I'll end up. I don't know where I am.'

Parker had a small orchard of late apples at the lower end of the farm and after dinner he took a horse and trolley and a long picking ladder and went down to gather them. He said what a nice day it was and how nice it would be if she came down, later, to give him a hand, and she saw him look with uneasy fondness at her hair.

'I'll see how I get on,' she said. 'I got to run down to the shop.'

For some minutes she watched the truck bump down the stony track that led beyond the oast-houses and the bullock-yard to the field and the orchard beyond. Then she found herself wondering what it would be like to be seeing him for the last time, and the thought exulted her. She found herself trembling as she went upstairs. She took a jug of hot water with her and in her bedroom she stripped herself and began to wash her face and body. She could still smell the dusky, clove-deep odour of her hair, fading a little now but still strong, and she longed for it to remain like that for at least that afternoon.

When she got into the new corset she stood for some time staring at herself in the glass. Then she put on her stockings and she stood up and stared at them too. It was the corset and the stockings, she thought, so sheer and smooth and shining, that did so much to alter all the tone and appearance of her body. The big bulges of her hips and stomach were carved down and held in a shell, and the veins of her legs, always like stiff blue worms, were hidden away. There was a division, too, between her breasts, instead of the sagging blown pillow that had always been there.

She was ready by three o'clock. As she went out of her bedroom she felt a sudden urge to make quite sure where Parker was. She climbed the stairs to the little balcony on the roof and looked down across the fields. She could see the tip of the ladder pointing up through the old red trees of apple and on the top of it the squat grey head of Parker, under the greasy hat, staring emptily like an owl. And once again she felt that she might be seeing him, that day, for the last time, and again the thought exulted her.

She walked up through the wood very slowly. Her body felt stiff in the unaccustomed corsets. She did not know quite what to do with her hands in the new white gloves and the heels of her shoes seemed to make her taller than she had expected.

It seemed like a strange accident when she saw the young keeper coming down the path to meet her. She felt nervous at the sight of him. The afternoon sun, low under masses of smouldering beeches, was dazzling in his eyes. She saw the blue fierce sparkle of them under ruckled brows.

He seemed suddenly unable to believe in the reality of her as she came up the path. He stopped and held his head sideways and squinted. Then he walked slowly towards her, imprisoned for a few moments longer in disbelief about herself, her new clothes, her new identity.

'It is you,' he said. 'I couldn't believe it. It is you.'

She felt herself trembling violently and could only say: 'It's my day off. You never saw me on my day off before.'

'I thought it was some stranger. I thought your day was Sunday.'

'It used to be,' she said. 'But now –' She hesitated as if she did not know quite how to frame what she had to say. She had lied so readily in the past that now it was not easy to tell the truth in a simple way.

'Will you walk part of the way with me?' she said.

'Which way?'

'I want to walk down to the village – I got to go down there for something –'

'I'll walk part of the way,' he said. 'I'd like to. You want to go by the bottom path? – it's nice in the sun.'

They walked for some distance on the dry chalk path, carved white into the hillside at the edge of the beeches, before she spoke again.

'I'm glad I saw you. I got something to tell you,' she said.

She looked down at her new black shoes. The toes of them were already dusty with the dry chalk of the path.

'That wasn't quite right what I said. It wasn't exactly right about my day off. That wasn't quite right.'

'No?'

'No,' she said.

'Is that what you wanted to tell me?'

54

'No,' she said. 'I wanted to tell you I was leaving there.'

He stopped on the path. His hands jerked across the front of his body as if for a moment he wanted to take hold of her.

'Is that true?' he said.

'Yes, it's true,' she said. Now when she told the truth she desired passionately to be believed. 'Why? – don't you believe me? Don't you believe it's true?'

'Yes,' he said. 'Only I wanted to be sure – I been waiting to hear you say that for a long time.'

Suddenly she knew that there was a change in him; she felt that they were drawing closer together. She did not speak for a long time as they walked along the path. She could only look down at her new shoes and see them growing cloudier every moment with the dust she raised from the chalk, and it was the shoes that made her speak at last.

'Look at my shoes – whatever do they look like? They look like nothing on earth.'

'I can dust them,' he said.

He began to take out his handkerchief.

'Not now. They'll be as bad again if you do,' she said. 'You could do them at the gate, couldn't you? Before I go down the road?'

'Are you coming back to-day?' he said.

'Yes.'

'How long before you come back?'

'I don't know,' she said. 'About hour. About that. I just got to go somewhere – I got to go down to see after that job I told you about. The one in the café.'

'Can I wait and take you back?'

'If you want to,' she said. 'Do you want to?'

They had reached the gate at the end of the path and in answer he pulled out his handkerchief and began to dust her shoes. She felt the touch of the handkerchief as it flicked against the silk of her stockings. She could feel his nervousness in the quick, too delicate movements of his hands, the nervousness exaggerating her own until suddenly she felt slightly giddy and put her hands on his shoulders.

For a few moments this first touch of him made her blind with excitement. She felt the beeches tremble about her like great orange breakers in the act of plunging downhill towards the sun.

When she could see clearly again she saw that he was standing upright. He was putting his handkerchief away in his pocket and speaking of how long she would be and how he hoped she would get the job and how he would meet her when she came back.

'Where will you meet me?' she said.

'Here,' he said. 'I'll watch for you coming up the road.'

She walked down to the café and ordered tea and sat drinking it slowly. She felt the flush of it heating her body, pounding through her blood and drugging her mind until there was no coherence in her thought. She felt mystified and wondering and slightly frightened of the change in her feelings exactly as she had been filled with wonder at the change in her body when she had first seen it, in its silky shell of corsets and stockings, in the glass.

When her thoughts at last began to come back to her, as she walked up the hill, they were very simple. In the night she would pack her things. In the morning she would be honest with Parker. In the afternoon she could go. In that simple way, she thought, there would be the end of Parker.

'I know where I am now,' she thought. 'I got to go while I can.'

She wanted to run the last hundred yards up the hill to where the young keeper was waiting under the long smouldering arch of beeches. Instead she plodded heavily forward, her big legs striking back to gain their power from the slope of the hill exactly as they had done in the days when she pushed the pram.

'Well here you are,' she said. 'Did you think I was never coming? Did you get tired of waiting?'

'Did you get the job?' he said.

'I got to go back another day.'

They walked for some distance along the path without speaking. Chalk dust rose again in small white puffs and gradually sprinkled its bloom on her shoes. He looked once or twice at her shoes before saying nervously at last:

'They're getting whiter and whiter. Shall I dust them?'

'In a minute,' she said. 'I'll find somewhere to sit down in a minute. It'll be easier like that.'

They were three or four hundred yards from the farm when she sat down on a beech-stump and put her feet and legs together so that he could dust her shoes. In the strong flat sunshine she was dazzled and could see nothing of the valley beyond his head. Half blind again, she was aware only of the movements, for the second time too quick and too delicate, of his hands about her shoes and ankles.

A moment later he was touching her legs. He was trying to say with coherence that he thought how beautiful she looked in the new shoes and the new stockings but the words, were too clumsy and too eager and suddenly the incredible stumbling fact of someone touching her legs and finding them beautiful was too much for her.

She got up and stood against him. As he held her she felt the entire front of her body turn molten and quivering. She shut her eyes against the strong gold glare of the sun and felt suddenly an extraordinary sensation of nakedness as she stood there on the open path and let him kiss her for the first time.

'I don't know what it is,' he said, 'but you're all different to-day. You look all different. Somehow it don't seem like you –'

'It's me all right,' she said. 'It's only the things I got on – the new things.'

She put her big awkward mouth up to him again, standing on the toes of her new shoes so that she could reach his face.

'Be here to-morrow,' she said. 'I got my things to bring. You'll be here, won't you?'

'What time?'

'Two o'clock.' She again had the queer uneasy sensation of nakedness, a strange impression of standing there starkly for the whole valley to see.

'Come into the wood,' she said. 'It's better out of the sun.'

In the shadow of the wood, under the coppery diffusion of light filtering down through crowds of turning leaves, she held his face in her new white gloves. Under their whiteness the skin of his face seemed a darker bronze than ever. He looked down at her with eyes transfixed in a deep and fond transparence, running his hands backwards and forwards over her head, and she wondered if he could smell the strong clove fragrance of her hair.

'How am I different?' she said.

'I don't know,' he said. 'Just different. I don't know how it is.'

She remembered how long she had wanted to be different and her wonder at being a new person in the eyes of some-one else became, for a moment, almost too much for her to bear. In her happiness she felt her eyes slowly filling with tears.

'Come and meet me to-morrow,' she said. 'You will, won't you? Come down to meet me – because to-morrow I'm coming for good.'

10

That afternoon she did not know at first, though she knew it afterwards, that Parker stood watching her as she came down the hillside from the wood in the strong flame of sun-light to the farm. For a few moments, as she walked into the kitchen, still dazzled by what had happened and by the fierce brightness across the hill, she did not even remember that he existed. She stood slowly taking off her gloves, pulling at the white fingers one by one, staring and dazed and not seeing the kitchen about her.

The sound of Parker's voice was like the grating of a rusty hinge.

'Where you bin? Where you bin gone all afternoon?'

'I been out – I had to go out somewhere,' she said.

Slowly the squinting rabbity-eyes enlarged, grey and then stark white in their distension, under the powerful disbelief of what he saw. She saw his mouth quiver in a jibber of astonishment as he stood by the table and stared. Like the young man he seemed unable to recognize in her the person he had known.

'What you done to yourself?' he said. 'Dulcie – what you done?'

In disbelief, touched by wonder, he started to come towards her. He moved in a groping sort of fashion, his hands slightly outstretched.

'Dulcie – it don't look like you – where'd you get them things?'

For a second or two she felt afraid of him. She was locked in fear by the enlarging, colourless, possessive eyes. Then, in her fear, before she was aware of it and before she could stop it, she said the natural thing:

'You give me the money for them – don't you remember? You give me the money –'

His sudden joy at remembering this simple fact made his eyes contract. They closed with a paroxysm of delight. When they opened again they seemed to flare warmly, almost with laughter.

'Gawd, so I did – I did, didn't I? I give y'it, that's right –'

'I better go upstairs and take 'em off,' she said. 'I got your tea to get. I don't want to get 'em mucky.'

'No,' he said, 'don't go. Keep 'em on – it's Saturday night. You keep 'em on. We'll go out somewhere –'

'I don't want to go out nowhere,' she said. 'I got work to do. I got things to do –'

He came close to her, putting his hands on her bare thick brown arms. His excitement, swollen by disbelief, seemed to suck greedily at recollection.

'Dulcie, I ain't seen you lately – you know, we ain't – You know what I mean – you know, like we used to.'

'I got to take my things off,' she said. 'I got to go upstairs afore I get 'em spoiled.'

'I won't spoil 'em,' he said. 'I got a right to see 'em haven't I? You got 'em for me, didn't you?'

59

'No!' she said. The word seemed to shriek itself, ejected by a pure shot of fear, before she could prevent it.

'No?' he said. 'You never?'

This time the sudden enlargement of his eyes was frenzied. They shone with glassy fury, swollen grossly.

'No?' he shouted. 'Then who the 'ell did you get 'em for?'

'Nobody. Nobody.'

'You got yourself up for somebody! Who was it?'

'Nobody. Nobody,' she said.

She started to back away from him. The one glove she had taken off had dropped on to the kitchen table and now she remembered and tried to grab it as she moved. It fell from the table and she stooped anxiously to pick it up. She became aware at the same moment of his hand swinging savagely in air, but whether to hit her or grab her or pick up the glove she never knew. She ducked and ran.

As she ran upstairs she heard the incredible stupefying shout:

'It's Albert, ain't it? I know – it's Albert – it's Albert, ain't it?'

She had forgotten Albert. She was so much at a loss to know what he meant by Albert that she stumbled against the stairs, grabbing the old-fashioned banisters to prevent herself from falling down. She clung there for a moment and then shouted back, angry:

'They ain't no Albert! They ain't no Albert! That's somebody I made up. They never was no Albert.'

His face appeared suddenly, thin mouth bared, at the kitchen door.

'No?' he said. 'They never was no Albert, wasn't they?'

'No, they ain't no Albert! I made it up –'

'I seen you!' he shrieked. 'I seen you up there! I seen you! – I bin watching all afternoon! – I bin watching!'

She saw the gleam of the shotgun barrel as he whipped it from behind the door with the air of violently conjuring it from nowhere. She slipped in her new shoes on the carpetless stairs as she ran. She began to sob again that there was no Albert, that it was only a name, a someone she had made up, and then a shot blasted the stairs and the landing, spraying the walls and the woodwork as she slipped in her new shoes for the second time.

It was the slip of her shoes that kept her down under the high trajectory of the shot. She fell against her bedroom door, opening it at the same moment, and threw herself inside. The second shot roared up the stairs, shattering the ceiling this time so that a hail of rotten plaster fell on the stairs and the bricks of the narrow passage below.

She locked the door and then pressed with all her weight against the long old-fashioned bolt, ramming it into place with a rattle that was like the echo of the second shot. In the act of doing this she used her ungloved hand and then she remembered the glove that had fallen from the table to the kitchen floor.

She began to cry. The recollection of the glove she had lost seemed suddenly more painful and more bitter than anything else that had happened. She lay face downwards on the bed in her new clothes, clenching with one gloved and one ungloved hand the edges of the canopy, sobbing with bitterness into the pillow, her face dark in terror.

From outside she heard the staggering crash of Parker as he lumbered up and down the stairs.

'You never thought I see you, did you?' she heard him yell. 'You never thought I could see – well, I see you, I see you – plain as daylight, you bitch!'

The word had the effect of pinning her down, in final paralysis, to the bed. It terrorized her more than the sound of the third shot, fired wildly across the landing with echoes of broken glass.

'You hear that?' he yelled. 'That's what bitches get! That's what you'll get too, you bitch – I can wait for you!'

She had nothing to say in answer. He fired a fourth shot and she heard it rake along the bones of the ceiling, bringing down a fresh hail of plaster.

'Y'ain't got nothing to say now, you bitch, have you? Well, that don't matter! – I can wait as long as you do. I can wait – I'm going to shut your mouth for you. I'm going to shut it for a long time. I can wait for you!'

She lay on the bed all night, not moving. Sometimes she heard Parker staggering about the house, yelling her name. There was no sound of another shot. In the deep darkness she could not sleep, but she cried from time to time as she remembered the glove she had dropped in the kitchen below. Then gradually her thoughts mounted and became an obsession about the glove, scared and fixed and predominant, and of how, sooner or later, by some means or other, she must go downstairs and find it again and go away.

II

Sometimes if the wind was right she could hear the chimes of the church clock coming up from below the hill and all through the next morning she lay on the bed and counted the hours by the strokes coming faintly through the quiet October day. Then she heard the ringing of bells for morning service and she knew that when they stopped it would be eleven o'clock. She still did not move as she listened to these things. Her thoughts remained obsessed, fixed always on the glove she had dropped and how, when two o'clock came, she would have to bring herself to face the business of unlocking her door and going downstairs and finding the glove and going away.

After the bells had stopped ringing for morning service, an enormous quietness came down across the hill. She found herself listening for sounds of Parker. It seemed strange not to hear the sound of a rusty cow-stall hinge and the clank of a half-door thrown back against a wall. It was odd that there were no sounds of cow-hocks whispering in straw or padding down through the flint yard to lower pastures. The mornings were always so full of these noises that they were as natural to her as the rising sun.

It was the deepening of this curious silence that made her turn over at last and lie on her back and listen more intently. It was strange that there was no sound of cows or feet in the yard, but it seemed stranger still that there was no sound of Parker. She thought of this for a long time. Then she began to think over Parker's habits and she remembered that he had a Sunday morning habit of cleaning his boots in the shade of the bullace-tree that hung over the hen-house across the yard. He liked to sit there for two hours or more spitting on the toe-caps of the boots and rubbing spittle and polish round and round with his fingers. The hens would cluck about him, scratching in the straw, and towards dinner-time she would take him a jar of cider and a glass and he would sit there drinking and polishing for another hour. That too, like the sound of waking and walking cattle, was as natural to her as sunrise.

Towards midday she got up for the first time and looked out of the window. It was possible to see the hen-house from the window of her bedroom but she saw at once that there was no Parker there and that the hens had not been let out for the day. There was no stir of anything about the bullace-tree except a blackbird attacking one of the fallen fruit as it might have attacked a snail, knocking it from side to side with its beak and exposing the raw green-yellow flesh. She saw then that the cow-barn had not been opened either and as she listened for the noise of animals moving she was aware of the silence amplifying and deepening all across the hillside in the late October sun. It seemed to cover everything with a soft close curtain and once again the wide low valley did not seem large enough to contain the deep discharge of her feeling, her fear that Parker was waiting, her joy at the thought of the young man, a profound cold wonder that such a thing could ever have happened to her. Then as she stood there she came aware, suddenly, of an extraordinary lessening of her fear. It was exposed as baseless in a flash that arose from a sudden twist in her mind.

'Because if I'm late he can come down all the way to meet me,' she thought. 'Then I'll be able to see him from the window. Then I can wave to him and he'll come down and nothing can happen.'

Her reassurance about this was so complete that she

began to get herself ready. In her mind the solution to things fell into place as simply as her scheme about the exploitation of Parker and Parker's passion for her and Parker's money had once fallen into place.

She stripped off her clothes. Her body was moist and creased from her night on the bed and her hair was pressed into a waveless mass that fell untidily about her neck. She washed her body as she had done the previous day, drying herself slowly, and then carefully putting back her clothes. She felt again the heavy pulse of satisfaction at seeing her body, coarse and floppy when naked, grow gradually into something that became smooth and silky and beautiful as she covered it with the corset, the stockings and lastly the dress and the shoes.

This transformation seemed even deeper with her hair. She combed out the waves, wetting them with the tips of her fingers and setting them back into place. During all this time, about an hour, she listened for the sound of Parker and for the sound of the church clock striking the quarters from below the hill, never hearing the one but always the other, her fear lessening and her confidence growing at the same time.

When finally she was ready she stood in front of the glass again, turning sometimes to see if the seams of her stockings were straight, touching the waves of her hair, thinking how wonderful it was that her legs and her hair were not as they used to be, thinking how much of herself was different.

'I'm all different,' she thought. 'He said I was. You're different somehow and I don't know how, he said.'

Just before two o'clock she stood at the bedroom window, watching the track that came down along the edge of the wood. She drew on her one glove slowly, remembering at the same time how she must pick up the other.

After a few moments she saw the young man coming down under the edge of the beeches. He had put on a new brown tweed jacket and she felt her heart give a pained start of joy, almost a stab, because he had dressed himself in his best clothes to come to meet her. She saw him come

down past the point where he had dusted her shoes and she
had taken him into the wood because her eyes were dazzled
by sun. She could see him with wonderful clearness and she
knew then the reason for that strange stark feeling of nakedness the previous day. It was her own queer premonition
that Parker was watching her.

Thinking of Parker, she listened for a final sound in the
house. When she could hear nothing she opened the window. The young man was standing about two hundred
yards away, waiting for her, and she began to wave her
hands. At first he did not see her and suddenly she had a
violent impulse to shout to him. She wanted to call his name.
Then she remembered that she did not know his name and
she felt herself framing the name Albert soundlessly with
her lips instead.

Suddenly he saw her and began to wave his hand. She
threw up her own hands in a great double gesture of
beckoning, repeating it excitedly. He seemed to understand
what she meant and began to walk down towards the farm,
baring his teeth as he laughed and waved his hand.

A moment later she pulled back the bolt of the bedroom
door and then turned the key and opened the door and
stood on the landing outside.

She began trembling again as she saw the shattered bones
of the ceiling and the mess of fallen plaster and its dust on
the stairs. There was still no sound in the house. With a
great breath she stiffened and found all her courage and
called:

'Mr Parker! I'm going now, Mr Parker. I'm saying good-
bye now, Mr Parker. I'm going home.'

She waited a second or two for an answer that did not
come and then she walked downstairs, crunching over
fallen plaster.

At the door of the kitchen she stopped again. 'Mr Parker,'
she said. 'I don't want to cause nobody no hard feelings but
I'm going now, Mr Parker. I'm going home.'

Parker was not in the kitchen. There was no sound in the
house. Then suddenly she saw her glove lying on the floor

of the kitchen, under the table, where she had dropped it the previous day.

She forgot about Parker as she ran and picked it up. All her life with Parker and her fear of him seemed remote and pointless in the moment of finding her glove. She felt quite calm again as she drew it on. She even found herself taking a final look at her hands, their coarseness hidden at last by the clean white kid, before she walked out of the kitchen for the last time.

She had hardly walked a dozen yards from the house before she heard the shot. A hundred yards away the young man threw his hands to his face and then clawed them away again, as if wrenching something from his eyes.

She was aware of wanting to scream his name. Then she remembered for the second time that she did not know his name and her mind began to scream 'Albert! Albert! Oh! my God, Albert!' though her lips did not utter a sound.

Above and behind her, from the top of the house, she heard a yell from Parker. She turned and saw him with the barrels of the shotgun levelled on the rails of the little balcony. She screamed again but the sound of her scream was shattered by the blast of the second shot. She saw the young man blown backwards in the act of wildly trying to wrench the pain from his eyes and then his body, convulsive like a rabbit's, turn over and at last lie still.

'Oh! my God, my God,' she said. 'Oh! Albert – Albert – Oh! my God.'

She stood still for a moment longer, weeping. Then she began to run, raising her white gloves in agony against the sky.

THE GRASS GOD

WHEN he stepped off the platform after another of those tiresome and long-winded village meetings in which people had argued for nearly two hours about the repairs of a little bridge he was pleased to see that everybody stood up again. He might have been a bishop leaving church. Some of the men, even the younger ones, touched their bare heads with their hands.

With amazement he could hardly bring himself to realize who and where he was. This was not the Russia of serfdom; it was not Ireland or Spain. He was not a bishop and these were not so many black peasant crawling beetles. This was England and these, he thought amazedly, were his people. They lived in his houses, paid his rents and – if it were not too harsh a term in these enlightened days – worked for him in his fields, on his four thousand acres.

'Good night, everyone,' he said. Before putting on his black homburg hat – he had been to town all day, and spring, enervating and sudden, had been rather exhausting there - he lifted it slightly. 'Good night.'

'Good night, Mr Fitzgerald, sir,' they said. Here and there a voice or two, he thought, said, 'Thank you.' He walked up the aisle between the chairs. 'Good night, sir. Good night.'

In the last fraction of a second before his hat touched his head, he saw, in the last row of chairs, by the door, the girl who had been watching him so closely throughout the meeting.

She was sitting in the extreme corner, alone, leaning her bare arms on a chair in front of her. In the entire hall she was the only person not standing up. When he had first noticed her it was for an entirely opposite reason – during his speech she had not once sat down: as if perhaps, he could not help thinking, she had wanted to see him better. During all that time he had seen her framed against the back wall, smoky-brown eyes watching him from under the yellow scarf tied across her head.

With some annoyance he thought that he did not like women who wore scarves on their heads; it was one of those sloppy frowsy war-time habits from which his wife never recovered. But as he looked at the girl she shook her head with a short upward toss so that the scarf fell free. He saw that she was quite young. Loosely the scarf fell about her neck like a kerchief and all the mass of her short thick brown hair was tousled free into a shining and fluffy ball, like the fur of a cat caught in a sudden wind.

She looked at him coolly, with a touch of arrogance that caught him off his guard. He felt a second spasm of annoyance – spring had really been rather too much in London – and something made him raise his homburg hat. She did not speak or move in reply. He was not even absolutely sure if she let herself be aware of that abrupt and quite courteous raising of the homburg hat. It was queerly impulsive on his part and it was all over in a second. He simply felt a small stab of anger and excitement go straight up through his throat and the next moment he saw that she was staring at the floor.

Outside he walked some distance before realizing how warm and beautiful the evening was: that the oaks, merely sprigged with buds a week ago, were now in full flower, lovely tasselled curtains of olive-yellow, already browned at the tips by the great burst of sun. All among them, too, down the road, big hawthorns were in solid pillowy white blossom, and he could smell the heavy vanilla fragrance of them as it weighted the warm wind. Spring seemed suddenly to have rushed forward, too warm, too leaf-rich, too flowery, out of the cold tight distances of a week ago. Luxuriantly the tender and dark, the sharp and misty shades of green had been kindled down the little valley, alder with beech, oak over hornbeam, all along the river and all across the wide tree-broken park to the line of white-cliffed hills that flared with miles of beeches.

He could not decide for some moments which way to go home. He stopped, looking for a little while at the country about him, the green spring world that seemed to be nothing but a series of wonderful fires of green and white quivering under the blue May sky.

He decided at last to go by the river. He had permanently locked the gates to the park some time ago. He carried the key of course: but the other way, by the small white bridge, where the river flowed shallow and bright through tunnels of purple alder and then into and out of a long, lily-padded lake, was very beautiful.

Running footsteps down the road behind him made him turn and look back as he opened the gate to the field; and a figure calling 'Sir, sir' in a sort of enlarged whisper came up by the wood.

'Yes, Medhurst,' he said, 'what is it?'

Dark, almost swarthy, with the tight southern forehead that was obstinately unpleasant, almost foreign, Medhurst touched his cap and said:

'I wanted a word with you, sir. If it's convenient, sir.'

Thick and unctuous and drawling, the voice had a touch of polite treachery in it that once again set Fitzgerald on edge. He had never quite got used to this foreign southern obstinacy, a feeling of treachery behind the politeness, the kow-towing, the touched hat.

'It was about the cottage, sir.'

'Cottage?'

'You remember you said you'd have one free in April, sir.'

'You must speak to Captain Fawcett,' he said. It was Fawcett's job to deal with this sort of thing; Fawcett was estate bailiff and it was entirely his business.

'It's no use speaking to Captain Fawcett, sir.'

'Oh?'

'He's terribly off-hand, sir. He's going to do this and he's going to do that and he never does.'

'I've never had any cause to think that Captain Fawcett was like that – '

'I'm living in a hut, sir,' Medhurst said. He stood tense, rather upright, glowering, almost menacing, it seemed, out of pure nervousness. 'We got no water. We have to go half a mile for water – '

'Where is this?'

'Down by Sheeracre, sir.'

'I never knew there was a hut there.'

'No, sir? It was the old shooting hut. It used to be half-way round the long beat. They used to have the shooting lunches there in the old days.'

'Wood or something?'

'Wood and tile, sir. It's half-tidy hut – '

'Then what are you cribbing about? There are thousands who haven't even huts.'

He half-turned away, curt with fresh annoyance. He heard Medhurst begin 'It's the water, sir. It's fetching the water for the baby, sir', and then down the road, a hundred yards or so away, he saw the girl again, coming towards him. She was taller than he had thought. She was swinging the yellow scarf, first in one hand and then in another, so that it flapped about her long slender legs almost like a bright apron in the sun.

Watching her, unaware of Medhurst, really not listening now, he experienced once again the curious stab of excitement in his throat. She walked with long supple strides, idly swinging herself a little from the waist, with a gliding easy movement of slender thighs.

'We had the tap froze up fourteen or fifteen times this winter. My wife was bad. We couldn't bath the baby – '

He nodded vaguely, as if really listening. He was aware only, at that moment, of the sharp and hollow noise made by the girl's footsteps as it beat up into the ceiling of thickening branches. Down through the wood, at the same time, the evening air was full of a warm throaty whistling of several blackbirds, lovely and bell-like, and beyond it the bubbling call of a cuckoo on the wing.

Presently as she came level with him he again made his own quick impulsive gesture with the homburg hat; and this time he thought he saw perhaps the slightest flick of her face in answer. Then she went past, still swinging the scarf in her hands, so that from the back the ends of it moved outwards from her long thighs like two yellow fins.

He was still thinking of how much taller and much more supple she was than he had first supposed when Medhurst said:

'Well, have I to speak to Captain Fawcett, sir?'

'I suppose so. Yes, of course.' What was one to say? On the whole estate there were a hundred and twenty people to house and now, after the war, as things were, it was very difficult to make up one's mind not to – 'I don't want to show favouritism,' he said. 'You understand?'

'You said the cottage up by the Thorn would be empty, sir – '

'Well, it may be. It may be. You must ask Fawcett. It's really his affair.'

'Yes, sir.'

Fitzgerald began to walk away: not, as he had intended, through the field, by the wood side, but along the road, towards the gates of the park.

'If you don't come to some arrangement with Captain Fawcett you must speak to me again.' He was simply talking automatically as he walked away. 'But after all it's a roof. Summer's coming on and you'll probably have to make do – '

'Yes, sir,' Medhurst said. 'Good night.'

'Good night.'

The thought of Medhurst went out of his mind swiftly, a moment later.

A hundred yards away the girl stood trying the gates of the park. He heard the hollow clatter of the iron handle. Once again an echo of the sound she made beat up into the curtain of spring leaves and again a whole chorus of blackbirds broke into singing in the wood, and a cuckoo, answered now by another, called in a mocking, floating sort of voice far down along the meadows.

Twenty yards away he called to her:

'I'm afraid the gates of the park are locked. I'm afraid there is no footpath now.'

She turned slowly and looked at him.

'There used to be. There always was.'

It struck him that there was a kind of accusation in that. Her eyes, dark and warm, like elongated buds, did not seem quite open. They held him in a narrow sleepy stare.

He had again already raised the homburg hat; now he took it off completely.

'It has been closed for more than a year. Nearly two years,' he said.

'It was always open.'

'At one time, yes.' Her long fine-skinned hands did swift little twisting tricks with the scarf. They reminded him of the mesmeric habit of a conjurer. He said: 'One has frightful bother with people. They abuse things. Trippers and all sorts of people used to come here and do heaven knows what damage – '

'It's an awful pity,' she said. 'It's very beautiful –'

He felt for a bunch of keys in his pocket.

'Did you want to go in? Were you thinking of walking through?'

'I was.'

'I could let you through. I'm going through myself – '

There was no change in the elongated drowsy stare of the eyes as she said: 'After all I think I'll walk back. It's late and perhaps there isn't time.'

'It simply isn't any trouble. I have the key. I always carry the key.'

He held his keys, a big silvery bunch, in one hand, trying to pick out the gate-key with the other. He had thirty or forty keys in the bunch. He knew it was a longish clumsy sort of key.

She stood apart, waiting, watching him try first one key

and then another, not speaking. He tried five keys that did not fit and then she said:

'So many keys and not the right one.'

'One uses it so rarely, that's the trouble – '

He clashed one key after another into the lock. Now his hat had become a nuisance to hold and he put it back on his head. He tried still another key but that too did not fit and he thought that, over his shoulder, she gave a short dry laugh, no louder than a gasp; but she was simply staring, drowsy as ever, when he turned and looked at her.

She began to say again that it did not matter; but he shouted through the gates towards the small gothic-windowed gate-lodge on the other side:

'Smith! Are you there? Smith! Are you there?'

A little knot-haired woman in a grey apron came running out of the house, a minute later, with the key.

'I'm terribly sorry, sir. I'm most terribly sorry. I didn't know. I didn't hear you – '

'Just want to walk through. I've mislaid my key somewhere.'

'Will you take the key, sir?'

'Yes, I'll take it,' he said. 'Give it me.'

Beyond the small white house, with its edging of wired-in scarlet-yellow wallflowers, began an avenue of white chestnuts, in full fresh blossom. On either side of it deep expanses of park-land, all grass, grazed by clusters of sheep and new lambs, spread out into distances broken by islands of silver birch, an occasional clump of pines and sometimes a single gigantic lime. On the hills beyond were miles of beeches, still flaring green in the evening sun.

'I noticed you at the meeting,' he said. 'Have you come to live here?'

'For a time. With my sister.'

'For a time?'

'For the summer,' she said.

He wondered for a moment what there could possibly be here, in a village of thirty houses and one public house and a shop selling nothing but stamps and the paltry rations of the brave new time, for a girl of her kind. At heart he really detested the village; he detested the little pigsty houses, the dreary shirts on the washing lines, the loafers by the pub-wall, the gossipers, the hat-touchers, the treachery, the southern lack of friendliness. It was nothing more than a gossip shop. And the little crust of society: the milkless wife of the retired naval fellow, commander or something; the dithering lunatic doctor, surgeon or whatever he was; and the horrible people who came to retire: dreary suburban-minded wretched people of no standing who waited for buses with lending-library books tied by little leather straps in their hands. There was a retired schoolmaster too, a real bolshevik, an out-and-outer; and a solicitor fellow, a counsel or something, who came at week-ends and poached such fishing as there was after the herons and others had finished with the trout stocks he put in. They were all divided into factions; they were all like horrible little weevils, feeding and boring away at everything with their trivial, insidious, killing gossip.

'Well, what do you make of our society?' he said.

'I only came last week.'

They were coming to that part of the avenue he disliked so much. There the chestnuts ended. Concrete tank bays, half ruined huts, old army kitchens and brick ovens blackened by fire, all overgrown by thick new nettles: that was all now as far as the big house, once painted so white that it could be seen shining from the hills five miles away.

'Then how is it you know about the footpath?'

'I used to come here as a little girl. My uncle lived here. My sister has his house now.'

'What was his name?'

'Russell,' she said. 'Did you know him?'

'No,' he said. 'I don't think so. I don't know people. Are you Miss Russell?'

'My name is Ferguson.'

'What else?'

'Sara,' she said.

In a gap beyond the chestnuts, where army hovels had

been demolished to earth level, there was a place from which you could look down on the entire green circumference of parkland. It was so vast that it was like a kingdom of virgin grass. A few buildings, his new cowsheds, white concrete with green roofs of an excellent new material he had discovered, could be seen on the far edge: a slightly discordant touch which summer, the great world of leaves, would presently conceal.

He stopped and, leaning on the iron fence, looked down on it. A nightingale was singing somewhere in the direction of the big empty house, but he was so absorbed by that long deep view, the sheep-grazed kingdom, the grass coming to lushness under hot May sun that the singing, the sweetness, seemed only a secondary matter.

Making signals with his hat, he began explaining things to her: 'You see we have everything under a system. Nothing haphazard. There are five-year leys and three-year leys and one by one we plough them in and then sow again. Grass is the key –' He broke off and looked at her. 'Boring you? I'm afraid grass is my pet thing. Sort of bible with me – '

'What are the little yellow and white numbers I see on all the gate-posts?'

'They're the field map-numbers,' he said. 'Down at the estate office we have a map. We colour each field a different colour. We give it a number. Like that we can never go wrong – '

She turned her face away from him; her cream soft neck tautened, making a single line from her breast to the tip of her hair as she listened.

'I think there's a nightingale singing up by the house,' she said. 'I've been listening –'

'I'm afraid I bore you with my leys and things,' he said. 'My grass.'

'Oh! no.'

'Not really?'

'Bore me?' She laughed; he saw her eyes sparkle quickly and beautifully and once again he felt his throat run hot as she held him for another second or two with dark eyes. 'You surely don't think so?'

She laughed again over her shoulder. Then she began walking on and he let her go: purely because now he could look from behind at the long lovely legs, the graceful sliding walk.

'Is the house empty? Don't you live here now?'

'Yes, it's empty.'

'It used to be so beautiful.'

He strode out to catch her up. Where the front lawn of the house had been, between great Lebanon cedars, there was a forest of rising nettles. Snow had broken down the big shining magnolia from the white south wall. Hadn't there been camellias there too at one time? He had a vague idea there had.

'You ought to live in it,' she said.

'Here? Oh! one can't. It's impossible. The labour alone – '

'It would be nice.'

'Oh! no. It's absolutely dog eat dog. One has servants to feed one and then servants to feed the servants and then servants still to feed – on! no, that's dead, all that. It's gone.'

'I like this house,' she said. 'I always have liked it.'

She stood quite still, looking up. The nightingale, unmistakable now, drawing out a long needle-note, almost too exquisite, was singing in the limes beyond the stable tower. The clock on the tower, which he always kept going out of principle, showed half past eight, and it reminded him to ask her something.

'Do you ride?' he said.

'Oh! no. Nothing like that.'

'What a pity,' he said. 'I was going to say that you would be welcome to ride here. Any time.'

'On the sacred grass?'

She laughed and he did not know, taken slightly unaware by the flash of her tongue in her open mouth and the sprinkle of light in the brown eyes, what to say in answer.

'No. I'd rather see the house,' she said. 'Could we see it? Could we go in?'

'To-night?'

'Oh! no. I mean some time.'

'There really isn't anything to see,' he said. 'Things are boarded up and so on.'

'Really it doesn't matter.'

'Oh! please,' he said. 'Of course. When would you like to go?'

'Whenever you have time,' she said. 'I'm free – quite free.'

'To-morrow?' he said. Again, hot and sudden, he felt stabs of excitement leap up through his throat. 'To-morrow evening?' She seemed, as he looked at her, suddenly identifiable with all the rising summer, exquisite and young, desirable as sunlight and slightly lush. 'When could you come?'

'About six?'

He nodded and then checked, in the same moment, an impulse to kiss her. He thought instead that all summer lay before him; it would be pleasant to know her all summer. Now it was only May; the leaf was hardly open on the tree.

'About six then,' he said. 'Here? I shall look forward to it very much.'

With flicks of one hand she swung the scarf; he hoped that to-morrow she would not wear the scarf.

'What about the gate?' she said. 'The key?'

'Oh! of course. I forgot.'

He held the key out to her; and for a second or two she held it at the same time, watching him with beautiful brown eyes that held him with something between gravity and the gentlest mockery.

'What shall I do with it?' she said. 'Give it up? Surrender it?'

'No,' he said. 'Keep it. For a time. Then you can let yourself in.'

'That's nice,' she said.

With high thrilling needle-notes the nightingale

continued to sing in the quietness about the house as she walked away down the drive between the ruins of tank bays and army huts; the evening flowered about him with an exquisite after-light that left on the limes, the candled chestnuts, the oak-tassels, the curdling boughs of hawthorn, and above all on miles of grass a tender lucid glow.

To the yellow scarf swinging away down the chestnut avenue he raised his black homburg hat for the last time, smiling as he did so. There would be all the time in the world to-morrow, he thought. The summer had hardly begun.

2

When he got to the small converted farmhouse on the north side of the park the door was open to the warm evening and he called inside:

'You there? Anybody there?'

His wife did not answer. It was not often that she did answer. But the woman who did the cooking appeared from the kitchen in her evening apron and said:

'Good evening, sir. Mrs Fitzgerald is out for the day, sir.'

There was never a day, he thought, when she was not out for the day.

'The day's getting old,' he said.

'Will you have dinner, sir? It can be ready when you like.'

'I'll have a drink first,' he said. 'Call me when you're ready.'

He poured himself half a tumbler of whisky and took it into the garden. Scarlet beans, budded low down with sprays of flower, were already curling far up a row of hazel sticks beyond the flower beds. He could see a great difference in them, as in everything else, since yesterday. Swallows were flying high in the warm air above the house, crying thinly, and on the single-storeyed wall beyond the dining-room, where there had once been only pigsties and a filthy little copper-house for boiling potatoes one day and

washing the next, the new *Gloire de Dijon* rose was already in
bloom, its fat flowers like stirred cream in the evening sun.

He had converted the pigsties into a sort of loggia and
summer-house. Everything had been done very tastefully;
and now it was not possible to believe that there, where the
rose flowered and where big pots of blue agapanthus lily
would bloom all summer, the hideous pigsties had ever
existed or that a family of half-gipsies had lived in care-free
squalor in the rest of the house. It showed what could be
done.

Walking about the garden, looking at the climbing beans,
the roses that had rushed into bloom in a day, the blue and
orange steeples of lupins, he felt once again that summer
was overflowing too fast, rising like a warm and delicious
torrent. He felt he wanted to hold it up, to make it per-
manent where it rose, before all the tender and dark and
fiery greenness deepened into solid June.

He wondered, without real thought, where his wife was.
It did not matter very much; he simply wondered. If
speculation had not bored him long since he would have
guessed with the doctor's wife, or with Mrs Naval Commander, or somewhere in the smug outposts of the local
metropolis, the railway junction, playing bridge. She
seemed to spend most days playing cards of some sort with
the wives of local doctors, local solicitors, local sheep-
breeders, local cattle auctioneers. Somewhere in that bleak
society there must be someone, he often thought, who
would not bore or chill or depress him but he had, so far,
never discovered them. In winter he arranged excellent
shooting parties; but he and his wife had for a long time
quarrelled with great unpleasantness as to whom they
should invite to them. The solution could only be, as he
once put it, that they should shoot each other's friends.

Part of the trouble with that simple and perhaps admirable arrangement was that he had very few friends for her
to shoot. He wandered about in the garden, drinking as he
walked. A breath of new perfume, from the edges of the
rock path, arrested him under a big gum-stained plum tree

he had left to shade the path, and underneath it he saw that already there were white pinks in bloom. He picked one of the flowers and smelled it, threading it into his button-hole. He saw too that already there were hundreds of small plums, like beautiful pale green grapes, all over the tree.

At this moment a voice called from the house:

'Dinner is ready if you are.'

He could not believe for some moments that it was not the voice of the cook who called. But with amazement he turned and saw, across the garden, that his wife had come home.

He felt at once moody and thwarted and did not answer. She stood in the small brick courtyard by the front door, wearing over her head, as always, the pale blue and white scarf with its scrawled views of Paris and tags of French quotations that he so hated.

She was thirty-nine, three years younger than himself; but her voice, cutting across the warm luxuriance of garden, was husky, almost rough, and it seemed no longer young:

'Are you coming? The soup's on the table.'

'I'm coming,' he said.

As he walked across to the house, slowly, he knew that he did not want to eat. A whisky or two, combined with evening, was enough. He wanted, really, nothing but that: the whisky, the evening, the scent of summer. It was an arresting, enchantingly pleasant thought that for him there would be, and always was, more summer than for most people. Summer, for him, rose and blossomed from four thousand acres. There, in his special province, everything he looked at and touched and smelled, grass and bluebells and corn and chestnuts and grass again and still grass, was his own. More even than a province, perhaps: almost a kingdom. From the big empty house down to the shooting hut that the fellow had bothered him about after the meeting, in a territory so large that he was really never sure about the outer girdle of its geography, summer was not simply on the grand scale. It was his own.

In the dining-room his soup was cold. After tasting it
once he got up and poured himself a second whisky and
stared at his wife.

'What else is there?'

'Chops, I think.'

'You think,' he said. 'If you were here you'd know.'

She did not answer and the chop, when it came, was
greasy and rather gristly; he sawed away at it, washing it
down with whisky.

'Couldn't we have pork again before the summer comes?
What do we keep pigs for?'

'I gave the last of the pork away.'

'Why?'

'You tired of it. You always tire of it. There's always too
much of it. I gave it away to friends – '

'Ah,' he said, 'how are the horse-stealers?'

It was on old drab dry joke of his to call her friends the
horse-stealers. She looked straight beyond him, not answering. She was getting rather fat in the face, he thought.
Perhaps it was because she lived awfully well and did nothing; perhaps it was simply the podginess of forty a little
before its time. Whatever it was he knew that he could not
endure it, now, for much longer.

'This meat is disgusting,' he said. He set down his knife
and fork.

Again she did not answer. He remembered the days,
before the war, before his father died, when splendid and
beautiful meat had come up, after being properly hung,
from their own slaughter-house. Pork and beef and lamb
and pheasant and veal: whatever one wanted had always
been at hand.

'Our situation's rather like the meat,' he said, 'isn't it?
It's bad and if we were honest we'd say we didn't want any
more.'

'I've never said I didn't want any more.'

'Because you're not honest.'

'I don't think it's a question of honesty.'

'No?'

How stupid it was; how stupidly idiotic to begin an argument like that. Only a tirade, an abusing match, already developing in the air, could possibly come from it. He gripped his hands under the table and determined that, if possible, he would stifle every single abusive word. It helped if you remembered that in a house as small as this the servants heard everything, and quite calmly, in a low voice, he said:

'Could I talk to you reasonably a moment? Will you listen?'

'I'm listening.'

'Will you finish it? Will you let me get out?'

'I've already said what I have to say about it,' she said.

In the quietness he could hear, through the open door, from far across the park, a series of haunting bell-like notes of a calling cuckoo as if they were chimes of a clock striking, and he recalled, for the first time since he had sat down, the girl swinging her scarf about her long slim legs under the chestnut trees.

'I'll provide the evidence and so on, the usual thing,' he said. 'I'll do everything.'

She did not answer. He noticed she had really not combed her hair properly before coming down to table, and he could see where it had been flattened and dishevelled by the scarf. That irritated him too; but another thought of the girl, so tall and slender and summery, pressed the irritation away. Someone like that: someone new and unknown and fresh, he thought. He remembered how, as she waved good-bye, he had let the thought of kissing her, to-morrow, all in good time, not too soon, lie pleasantly in his mind. All his anticipation about her had seemed to tremble gently on the very edge of summer.

'There's nothing you need do,' he said, 'really. I'll provide all that's necessary – '

'Had you someone in mind?'

She had finished her chop to the last; her mouth, rather too magenta with lipstick, shone thick and greasy as she looked up.

'No,' he said.

'I thought perhaps you might have.'

'Why?'

'It was just a thought.'

The young girl who helped in the kitchen came in, a moment later, to clear the plates away. He stared at the table and his wife said:

'You have a pink in your buttonhole. That's nice.'

'Summer has come all of a sudden,' he said.

Into this interval of polite conversation his wife pressed a new pin-prick of irritation:

'What's for afters, Margaret?'

In a soft voice the girl said that there were gooseberries and his wife repeated, as if he had not heard it and it were a circumstance of exceptional joy:

'The first gooseberries. Isn't that marvellous?'

There could be nothing marvellous about it, he thought. He detected too that south-country, half-cockney expression, so cheap in some way, by which afters signified dessert. Everything about his wife now fused into a central irritation: the scarf, the uncombed hair, the greasy mouth, and now the way she spoke, the words she used, her jubilation concerning commonplace things.

'Custard with the gooseberries?' she said.

'I don't want either,' he said.

'As you like.'

'I want to get this thing cleared up,' he said.

He stared at her grimly, tightening his hands under the table.

'If I told you I hated you would that make any difference?' he said.

'No.'

'Would anything make any difference?'

'No.'

She was eating gooseberries bathed in yellow custard. She ate with a certain hearty lustiness, like a schoolgirl, and slops of yellow stuck to her magenta lipstick. She fixed him calmly with her pale grey eyes and said:

'I'm quite content with things. I like the house and I have friends.'

'The horse-stealers,' he said, 'spongers.'

'Perhaps they don't like you, either.'

'They like what I have,' he said. 'That's what they like.'

He got up to take a little more whisky from the side table. As he stood drinking it, not knowing quite what to say, the girl came in from the kitchen and said:

'Excuse me, sir, there's someone to see you.'

'Who?' he said. 'Who? I'm having dinner!'

'Don't shout at the child,' his wife said.

'I am not shouting,' he said and knew that he was. He walked out of the open door into the garden, banging his glass on the table as he passed.

A figure was waiting at the small latch-gate by the summer-house and as it turned he said, loudly:

'Medhurst. What do you want?'

'I been to see Captain Fawcett, sir.'

'I'm having my dinner. Why the hell have I to be dragged out to listen about Fawcett?'

'Captain Fawcett says he spoke to you about this cottage seven or eight times, sir.'

'I don't recall it.'

'Everybody knows you're rather forgetful, sir, and I daresay you forgot it.'

'Forgetful? Forgetful?'

'You're away a lot too, sir. You're away and you don't know what goes on.'

'What does go on? Tell me.'

'Well, sir,' Medhurst said. 'Well –'

'Well what?'

'There's a lot said, sir. There's a lot of feeling.'

'For Christ's sake about what?'

'One thing and another,' Medhurst said. 'One thing and another.'

He felt his heart raging inside him at the thought of the accumulating evil pettiness about him, at the vague insinuations of disloyalty and dislocation. There was no

doubt that here and there the damn bolsheviks were working their way in. It was not like the old days, when one had
loyalty and trust and decency and continuity of service.
Now there were always labour troubles, dissatisfaction, some
feeling of unspecified unrest. He was about to say something about this when Medhurst said:

'I don't want to keep you from your dinner, sir. But I'd
like to ask you something.'

'What?'

'Will you come and have a look at this hut to-morrow?
I don't think you've ever been down –'

'All right,' he said. 'I'll come.'

'Very well, sir. You come down.' He opened the gate,
went through it and stood the other side of it. 'About six?
I'll be home from work and had a wash by then.'

'All right,' he said. 'I'll be down.'

It was only when Medhurst was twenty or thirty yards
down the road that he remembered that, after all, he could
not go at that time. He remembered his delicious feeling of
anticipation about the girl in the yellow scarf: and how,
to-morrow, they were going to explore the house together.

Then as he got back to the house he heard the sound of
a car being driven away. Harshly the gears clashed up the
quiet road, and he knew that, all too soon, before he could
speak again, his wife had gone. It was almost dark and he
was alone now with the whisky, the scented garden and the
big empty space of the park, all grass, beyond.

His wife's name was Cordelia: and somehow he had never
quite come round to that, either.

3

Every morning in spring and summer he was up by seven
o'clock in order to make, sometimes in a jeep, sometimes a
small dog-cart, a tour of the estate. It was wonderfully
pleasant, often a tonic of exhilaration for him after a bad
evening with Cordelia and the whisky, to drive into deep
woodland roads, under high banks of primrose and bluebell

and bracken, through plantations of birch and sweet-chestnut, in and about the little valley. There he had almost everything; on those four thousand acres there were endless variations. Hop-gardens on the south-west slopes, from which on fine days you could see the line of sea, flanked old and excellent cherry-orchards and tasselled plantations of hazel-nut. In copses about the park rhododendrons had been planted for game-cover and from under startling magenta fires of flower cock-pheasants would come serenely stalking, themselves on fire with flames of brilliant scarlet and green and blue. On the lake water-lilies, both yellow and white, grew in thousands and wild duck inhabited the small upper islands of sallow. Where the cherry-orchards finished their snowy blossoming there were many acres of pink apple and then, in high summer, the great fragrance of limes about the park. The largeness and width of it embraced everything, from prize cattle to a white peacock or two that still roamed about the old wild lawns behind the big house, among the rose-pink camellias he had forgotten.

It had not always been so large. At the time of his father's death there had been not more than two thousand acres. They were the slump days. His father had been rather a mean but in many ways admirable landowner, conservative and human, liked and feared, of the old nineteenth-century school. Everything had been cautiously solid, thorough, unscientific perhaps, but profitable. Labour had been cheap; men were two a penny. Twelve gardeners, with a number of apprentice boys, had raised delicious things in the old walled gardens and hot-houses sheltered from cold winds by Atlantic cedars. Peaches and asparagus were always ready to perfection before their time; there were always amaryllis and gardenias and carnations and orchids for the house. A loveliness flourished, unhurried and quiet and prodigal, that had never come back and now never would.

His father could not have died, in a sense, at a better time. The slump was grim and stubborn; estates everywhere were breaking up. His father had been a man who believed in eating his apples only from the trees he had.

Solid entrenchment, capital sagaciously invested, had built up an estate that was like a bastion. If times were bad you did not venture out beyond it; if they were good you still remained at home. That was what prudence and capital and sound sense and foresight gave as their reward: an antidote of comfort against evil days, another spread of butter for the good.

His father, in consequence, had never bought land. Expansion, like spraying fruit trees, was not in his philosophy. But after he had gone it was different. All about the edges of the estate were pieces of land, either other estates or little farms, that the slump had beaten into decay and that were ripe for selling. And so another fifty or a hundred acres were added here; a hop-garden or an orchard there; a number of useful little farms, many pieces of woodland and another mile of stream. Where other people were shedding land against the evil of the times, the slump and the threat of war, the son acquired it. And he went on acquiring it, cheaply, thoughtfully, and as it turned out wisely, until the beginning of the war.

As a landowner, a farmer, though young, he did not go to the war. It was after all not necessary; a modern army did not merely fight on its stomach; at least six, and later ten or more persons were needed to keep a single soldier in the field or a pilot in the sky. Not everybody was needed for fighting. So he had stayed at home, in the country, raising food that everyone needed, putting the plough firmly back into soil that had never seen a share for centuries, unlocking richness.

About that time too he had closed the house in the park. He had never liked that dog-eat-dog existence, with servants feeding on servants, butlers lording it over underlings, pocketing the perquisites of the pantry, and he had never really cared for hot-house flowers. Orchids and gardenias and poinsettias, all so un-English and precious and unreal, were symbols of a world he found he could give up without a flicker of regret. Soil and grass, things of depth and substance and reality, replaced them; and gradually he had brought to them, to grass especially, a scientific interest that was more than a theoretical passion. It became a creed.

As he drove in the jeep through the park on the following evening he decided to make a detour to the south side, to where, on a two-acre strip, he conducted trials on thirty or forty kinds of grass and clover variations. Soils deficient in nitrates, in limes, in potash, or whatever it was, were marked off in oblongs, to be given their trials of grass in endless permutations.

He stayed for a short time looking with pleasure and pride at the patterns of delicate and brightening green. It had been another beautiful day; there was a warm trembling everywhere of rising grass and leaf and flower. Flies were dancing and you could feel in the air, in the blackbird throatiness, the cuckoo mockery, the whole deepening pulse of summer.

Then as he drove the jeep back across the park, already quite dry and hard from the heat of sun and yellow now in brilliant varnished stretches of buttercups, he saw a man in shirtsleeves working out on the grass. He remembered then his plan of soil-testing the entire estate. That gigantic task, to be recorded in time on a great coloured map that would hang in a special section of the estate office, was something he supposed not one farm in a thousand, in England at any rate, had ever done. In America of course they did this sort of thing; America was soil-plotted. They were ahead of us there.

He stopped the jeep and walked across to talk to the man who, with an implement like a large auger, was making trial borings into turf.

'Hullo, Pritchard,' he said. 'How does it go?'

'Good evening, sir.' The man, quite young, in his shirt-sleeves, was sweating heavily. 'Warm. See that?' He held up the auger, with its spiral of pale brown soil, crumbling away hairy rooted earth with his fingers. 'Dry. As if there'd never been any rain. Ever.'

'Extraordinary.' The dry rainless spiral of earth crumbled

like dusty brown cake, sprinkling the tall buttercups. 'How is it here? What have you got?'

'Sandgate beds. Not too good. You've got signs of spring water at twenty-two inches nearly everywhere. I'll let you see.'

Pritchard screwed the auger down into earth, and then with a swift jerk wrenched it up again.

'See the little rusty patches? like veins?' He thumbed away iron-coloured crumbs of soil. 'That's your water.'

'Bad?'

'Typical. Water everywhere.'

Fitzgerald knew that it meant more drainage schemes. They were very expensive; but he knew too that they had to be done and that he would come to them gradually too, all in good time.

'I'm glad you're having this done, sir.'

'Yes,' he said.

'It seems amazing when you come to think of it that we walk about on land and haven't the slightest idea what goes on underneath it.'

'Yes.'

'I mean for example the water. You'd say the land here was bone dry. Never a drop of moisture in it. Yet there it is – water everywhere, all the way down water seeping through.'

'It's a revelation,' he said.

Presently he said good-bye and got into the jeep and drove up through the buttercups to the house. It was striking six when he parked the jeep by the blackened and ruined army huts. A soft yellow bloom of buttercups had been beaten up and lay softly on the wheel-hubs, and by the army ruins crowds of white nettles were in flower.

Down the avenue he could not see the girl.

A curious feeling of disappointment suddenly gnawed at him as he stood there waiting. He had thought of the whole affair, the previous day, as something deliciously casual, almost offhand. He had not even wanted her, as he often wanted other women, out of loneliness, or in pleasure-spite against Cordelia, who would neither go nor let him go.

But now, as he walked up and down by the ruins and the nettles, he hated the idea that, after all, the girl was not coming: that she was going to let him down. It was not simply that he was used to people doing the things he wanted. It was something else; it was something not expected, an annoyingly elusive development he could not define.

Then suddenly he heard her call. He turned and, in a startling moment of surprise and pleasure and irritation, saw her coming from behind the big cedars at the side of the house. His irritation arose from the fact that she was once again wearing the same yellow scarf: this time tied over her head.

Even that irritation melted as he watched the long slender legs swinging through the grass. To-day he was not wearing his hat and he simply lifted his hand to greet her. She waved her hand too and he saw that she carried in it a spray or two of rose-pink flowers.

'Camellias,' she said. 'I found the trees.'

'For a moment I thought you were not coming.'

'I wanted to get here first. I wanted to see it in any case, whether you came or not.'

'Did you think I wouldn't come?'

She seemed to consider this question for a moment. Half smiling, dark eyes again like elongated buds above the shell-like rosettes, so pure and waxen, of the camellia flowers, she said:

'No: I knew you'd come.'

Together, then, they began to walk up to the house.

'Where did you find the camellias? It's late for them.'

'At the back,' she said. 'Don't you know? You mean to say this is your house and yet –'

'I always fancied they grew this side, on the wall.'

'Curious man,' she said. 'Don't you think they're beautiful?'

He said yes, he thought they were beautiful. It had been many years since he had seen them or even since he had been into the house; and as he drew out his great bunch of keys and started to unlock the front door he said:

'I warn you it's an absolute shambles. There's nothing to see.'

A moment or two later, as he pushed open the big white door, it was possible to see how true that was.

He stood inside the big hall-way with the girl, looking up at the stairs. They were elegant and wide and had once been white. Pictures had hung on the high walls. He remembered, as he looked at the dark unfaded rectangles left by them, that they had been very solid and sombrely ancestral. They had given tone. But now all pictures, all tone, and even half the stair balustrade had gone. An army had, in the army way, availed itself of several stair-rails, an odd window ledge, the shelves that had once held tea-services on either side of the fireplace. It had left blackening boot marks like dark repeated bruises all the way up the naked stairs.

'You see,' he said.

He half turned away as if to go out again.

'What's in here?' she said.

'It was the drawing-room,' he said. Now it was marked 'Company Commander: Keep out.'

Blinds with yellow silken tassels were drawn at the windows. By the side of the fireplace a few notices in typescript were still pinned, daily routine orders or things of that sort, and one or two sheets had fallen into the hearth, where showers of soot, pocked with rain, had covered them.

'You see, it's all gone,' he said. 'I told you.'

'Upstairs,' she said. 'What's up there?'

He knew that it could only be the same upstairs. Walking carefully, trying the bare blackened treads as he climbed, he led the way upstairs. A smell, dusty, sun-dried, greasily and stalely old, met him everywhere. No colour, even where the wallpaper of the main landing had once been a broad pattern of silver and chicory, remained now. Dust and time and the army locusts had eaten it away.

The effect of her walking into this, fresh and lovely, the spray of pink camellias in her hands, was startling to him as he turned and looked back down the stairs. Once more a leap of excitement, accompanied by the slightest wave of impatience, went through him as he watched her.

She looked up. What he felt was evidently clear in his face and she said:

'Something wrong?'

'No,' he said. 'Nothing wrong.'

It was useless, he thought, going through the whole business, quite pointless and silly, walking along empty dust-grey floors, from the derelict desert of one room to another. There was nothing to be got from it and his feeling of impatience grew. However much he wanted to kiss her he could not kiss her there among the ghost-ruins, on the broken stairs, in the sun-stale dustiness of a dead world.

He was glad when, on the second storey, they reached the far side of the house, where smaller rooms, one from a central balcony, looked out over what had once been the garden below. He had completely forgotten the geography of that floor, once the servants' quarters, until suddenly she opened a door and cried out:

'But there's furniture in here. A bed and things –'

'Odd,' he said. 'It can't be. Good Lord!'

A single divan bed, with a bentwood chair, a kitchen table, and a little strip of carpet furnished the room that opened through French windows on to an iron-railed balcony. He stood for a moment in the doorway, puzzled by it all, and then he remembered.

Here, in blitz days, fire-watchers had brewed tea and kept a look out for the enemy and slept. From the little balcony they had been able to see all across the gardens, to the deserted hot-houses, and along the valley. He remembered it all: the ladder out on to the roof, the rows of fire-buckets, the shovels, the sand-bags, and the sand. Queer how one forgot these things. He had even had his own estate fire-engine, with seven or eight trained men and organized practices and a decent run of hose. It had been rather fun.

He opened the French windows. For some moments he

stood half in and half out of the room, looking at the wilderness of cedars and nettle, lilac and thistle below. The room had a western aspect and now warm sun poured in, heavy with scent from many old sweet lilac trees.

Turning to explain about the room, its bed and its fire-watchers, he found the girl just behind him, looking across the valley. Once more the scarf roused in him a sharp sense of excited annoyance, and once more she caught the swift look of it in his face.

'What is it –?'

'Just the scarf,' he said.

'Don't you like it?'

'I hate it.'

He took the scarf between his fingers and began to untie it. She shook her dark hair free as he pulled the scarf away and threw it on to the little bed. A half-smile on her face parted her lips very slightly, as if she were going to say something, and her long body was pressed against him, close and supple, as he kissed her.

'Did you bring me here to do that?' she said.

'You wanted to come here.'

'Was I the only one?' She smiled, holding her lips up to him a second time. He wanted to take her quickly, in a sudden rush of over-exquisite feeling, but she said softly: 'Careful of the camellias. They're too lovely to spoil. Let me put them on the bed.'

She laid the camellia spray on the bed, beside the scarf, with gentle and almost ironic care.

'There,' she said. 'Now my hands are free.'

Smiling again, she let the outward gestures of her hands fall away. It gave an impression of slight mockery to her whole body as she leaned back against the side of the open window, eyes half-closed. The sun on her eyes turned them once again to the shape of long half-open buds; and when her mouth opened slightly, quivering with what he felt might have been either excitement or amusement, he bent to kiss her again.

There was a curious mixture of emotion behind that

second kiss, or perhaps lack of it, that baffled him. She seemed one moment to stand there, arms open, free, ready to offer herself like something on a plate; and then the next moment she was gone, withdrawn, cool and charming, beautiful but shut away.

'Queer how you found this room,' she said.

'Oh! no – I had no idea –'

'It's lovely. I like it. No garden, no gardeners, nobody here –'

'It was used during the war by fire-watchers.' He began to explain it with seriousness. She smiled again and out in the garden he thought he heard the first clipped charring notes of a nightingale. He saw her listening too; and when she broke away to lean against the iron railing of the little balcony he let her stay there for a moment or two alone, looking at the shape of her body as it curved forward, the legs long and firm, the thighs a little heavier and rounder in shape than he had thought them to be, sleekly pressing against the silky material of her dress. He could not resist the notion of touching her there, where the full roundness filled out the skirt; and it occurred to him once again how pleasant the growing summer was, how pleasant it could be there with her, in light, exquisite, and not too serious moments like this: quite alone, quite exquisite, quite without responsibility.

The nightingale, breaking away from the first short charring notes, began to sing with high sustained flutings of clear ecstasy and the girl said: 'There she goes again.' All this time she did not seem to be paying any attention at all to the regular gentle caressing of his hand across her body. The strange tangled wilderness of great trees and nettles, billowing hedges of lilac, blackberries strangling catalpa-trees, elderberry swarming over beds of dying rose, seemed to fascinate her instead into a long oblivious stare.

Suddenly she said: 'We're not alone after all. There's somebody walking about behind the cedar trees.'

'Where?'

'You can hear it,' she said.

The evening was so still, quite without wind even up there at the top of the house, that he could hear the shuffle of dry footsteps, exactly as she said, among dead leaves and grass behind the cedar trees.

'No one comes up here,' he said. 'The gates are locked.'

'There's someone. A child or something. You can see them now.'

A ghost-like trail of something white, behind the low black cedar branches, became one with the dry shufflings of feet among grass and leaves.

'It's a peacock,' she said. 'A white one.'

'I thought they'd been taken away –'

She leaned forward to watch. Delicate and snow-white and finicky, the white peacock trailed slowly away, half-hidden, a ghost-bird in the grass; and as she leaned forward he let his hand curve upwards round her body. But once again she seemed as if she did not notice it; or as if it did not interest her.

'Peacocks and camellias and rooms in the tops of houses,' she said. 'Do you know what you *have* got?'

'One can't live on peacocks and camellias and things,' he said. 'I'm a farmer. A business man, a landowner.'

'This lovely house,' she said.

'Oh! lovely,' he said. 'Wonderful. Forty servants and a hundred tons of coal every winter –'

'I like it,' she said. 'I like it here. There's something about it.'

'Would you like to come again?' he said. He moved his hand, touching and turning her body so that it moved upward and round to him. 'Often?'

'Often.'

In that moment, as he prepared to kiss her again, she turned suddenly and drew him into the room.

'Not there,' she said. 'I don't trust anyone. Not even the peacock. And anyway I must go.'

'Please.'

'I must go.'

'I had a call to make on one of my men and I was going to ask you if you'd come along –'

'To-morrow,' she said.

'All right,' he said. 'Shall we meet here to-morrow and then go –'

'No. Let's go first, wherever it is, and then come back here.'

He kissed her again; and there, by the bed, with the sun coming in a long warm shaft through the open window, he received in return the same restrained, cool, withdrawn, and yet half exquisite sort of kiss that had baffled him before. In the garden the nightingale was charring and whistling on high notes. The white peacock, like a bird sleep-walking, rustled with dry, almost harsh echoes through dead leaves and grass. The girl picked up her scarf and the spray of camellias from the bed. And as he moved to kiss her for the last time he touched by accident, for a second, the too delicate waxy flowers; and the rosette of petals, breaking like round pink wafers, fell to pieces.

'Careless man,' she said.

4

He could not help feeling that there was far too much fuss, the following evening, about the water-supply for Medhurst.

Twice, as the girl sat waiting in the jeep under the narrow arch of hazels that spanned the stone track leading through gated copses to the old wood-frame shooting hut, he stepped out the distance from the back door of the house to the well about which there had been so much complaining. It was not more than fifty yards.

'You said the thing was a hundred yards away,' he said.

'You git a morning with a foot of snow,' Medhurst said, 'and it seems like half a mile.'

'It seems, it seems,' he said. 'But the fact is it's fifty yards.'

Medhurst, dark and glowering, in his shirtsleeves, stood watching Fitzgerald pace the field. His wife, a sort of half gipsy creature, Fitzgerald thought, with scrawny black hair and a black blouse pinned across her hollow chest with a safety pin, stood at the back door nursing a greasy-nosed child of eighteen months naked except for a rag of overall.

'Well, let's leave the question of how far the water is,' Fitzgerald said. 'What about the water? Is it good?'

'It's quite good, sir.'

'You've no complaints about the water?'

'No, sir.'

He stood looking at the shooting-hut. Perhaps, some-times, under pressure of events, of business, of time itself, he was rather forgetful; he granted that. But now he clearly remembered the hut. As a boy he had come with his father on shooting parties there. It was a convenient half-way house on the perimeter of the estate as it then was. He re-membered the little hut crowded with shooters; the smell of good tobacco, the sharp rich reek of whisky, the aroma of fatty delicious hams fresh from under starchy napkins in shooting baskets. He remembered the beaters with plates of good beef and glasses of golden beer standing about on autumn mornings under the yellowing boughs of hazel and hornbeam; the clack of voices in the wintry woodland air.

It had been very pleasant in those days; the shoots were not the same now.

'Well,' he said, 'what about the house?'

'Well, there it is, sir. You see for yourself.'

Of course he saw. It was an oblong asbestos-and-frame affair with a brick porch and chimney and square sash-windows. A tiled roof, once red but now a pleasant shade of ochre-green from a heavy growth of lichen, sat on the place like a crumpled and sagging hat. Paths of coal ashes led about a garden of gaunt cabbage stalks, undug as yet after winter, and a line of grey washing hung by the wood-shed.

'How many rooms have you got?' he said.

'One,' Medhurst said. 'You see there's one big room.'

'Is that all?'

He supposed there never had been more than that one

large room; he supposed too that there ought to have been some sort of conversion of the interior, but he could not remember. His only memory of it was something extraordinarily aromatic and pleasant and snug.

'You like to have a look inside for yourself, sir?'

'If that's convenient.'

'I'd like you to have a look, sir.'

At the door, as he followed Medhurst, the wife stood apart, dangling the greasy snoffling child in the air so that he caught a glimpse of naked limbs, unwashed as it seemed for weeks. Her face too, young but colourless, was ditched in its neck wrinkles by earth-dark grime. Her shoes were tied with string; and she stared dully, half vacant, as he removed his hat before going through the door.

Inside, half as he thought, it was not precisely as Medhurst said. A kitchen with sink and oil-stove, from which led off a small scullery with copper, made in the first place two rooms. Then there was a third, divided in turn into three by screens of plywood that did not reach to ceiling height: making a sitting-room with two bedrooms beyond.

'I thought you said there was one room,' he said.

'Well, rightly it's one, sir.'

'I don't get that. By my computation it's five.'

'By rights it's one, sir. It always was one and it's no different –'

'Well, one or five –'

He looked about him, depressed, angry, resentful that his snug recollection, aromatic with hams and whisky and tobacco, had been so vilely extinguished by the frowsy filth, the uncleared table, the couch piled with bed-junk, the floor littered with wreckage of gum-boots and sacks and an occasional battered toy. Icily, yet raging inside, he said:

'What are your complaints about the place?'

'Well, first there's the water –'

'You said you had no complaint about the water.'

The woman, still dangling the child, came and stood staring in, with open mouth, at the door:

'We gotta sleep in two rooms, we gotta sleep in two rooms –'

'The three of you?'

'No, sir: six,' Medhurst said. 'You see we got two more boys and a girl, sir. They're growing up. That's the trouble.'

Fixed by the dark and groping stare of the woman, Fitzgerald was shaken by a short repugnant wave of sickness. He was repulsively amazed by the thought of physical contact. Sleep, children, the exquisite nature of women and love: he could not grasp that here, among the dark fibres of this revolting and infuriating existence, these things had ever had the remotest reality.

'We gotta sleep in two rooms, we gotta sleep in two rooms –'

'What are you making now, Medhurst?' he said.

'Just under the five, sir.'

'You get the allowances?'

'Yes, sir.'

'That's another fifteen, isn't it?' he said. He was not waiting for an answer. 'Your wife – surely she makes a little? Hopping and pea-picking and that sort of thing? And the boys? They make something?'

'Yes, sir.'

His final revulsion spat itself out:

'Then what in heaven's name are you cribbing about?'

While Medhurst stood flushed and speechless, the wife began to whine by the door: 'We gotta sleep in two rooms –'

'First you pretend it's one room. Then it's two. In point of fact it's five.'

'I suppose it is, sir.'

'Of course it is. You twist it to make one. Just as you twist the water. What do you want me to do?' He was trying to make for the doorway, almost shouting. 'Look at it. Look at it for yourself. It used to be a charming, civilized little place – it used to be tolerably decent –!'

His own words seemed to eject him past the unwashed woman and the snoffling child, through the unwashed kitchen. Behind him he heard the grousing mutter of

Medhurst's voice throwing a broken word or two of final complaint at him down the coal-ash path. In his rage an awareness of another exquisite evening, all gold-floating light, lovely with oak-flower and tenderly drowsy with bluebell scent from below crowded hazels, was almost too much to bear.

It occurred to him then, as he walked back to the jeep, that he had been longer than he thought. The girl was no longer waiting. For a second or two he stood in the narrow lane, his rage slowly declining and leaving in its place the queer haunted sense of gnawing disappointment he had experienced the previous evening: the distant, not wholly tangible fear that somehow, in an odd casual moment, when she chose, she would let him down.

He was relieved and glad to see her coming along the woodland path under the hazels.

'I thought I'd lost you,' he said.

'Again?' She smiled. 'A flower for you.' She stood close to him, so that her body almost touched him, threading a pink-white bottle-brush flower into his buttonhole. 'An orchid.'

His dislike of those other orchids, the exotic purple leopard mouths his father had been so fond of growing, crossed his mind; but he forgot it immediately.

'We are being watched,' she said.

She was being expressly gentle and careful, almost deliberately finicky, with the flower.

'The people from the house,' she said. 'Now the stories will begin.'

From the corner of his eye he saw Medhurst, the woman and the bare-buttocked child against a background of gaunt cabbage-stalks, ash-paths and grey washing by the wood-shed.

'Stories?'

'I am threading a flower into your buttonhole. I am riding in a jeep with you. What more do they want?'

His revulsion at the fetid depravity of the little house came rushing back. Hatred, both for the malignant shattering of recollections pleasantly stored from childhood and for the mere existence of the three unwashed people now staring at him, darkened his mind.

'They're the people who govern us,' he said. 'They're the power now. Look at them. The masters.'

Only a little later, struck once again by the beauty of the evening – the track curled upward through old orchards of late apple still in deep pink blossom – he calmed down. He almost forgot it all. The scent of apple-blossom was so soothing and sweet in his nostrils that he began to drive more slowly, with one hand: the other on her knee.

'What about the stories they'll tell of you?' he said. 'Don't you care?'

'I'm only here for the summer.'

'Long enough for the horse-stealers and mongrels,' he said. It was unlikely she would understand that expression; but he did not explain it. 'Shall we go up to the house?'

'I love it there.'

A final mutter of his discord came back:

'They tell nothing but lies, these people. They whine and lie and touch their caps and all the time they hate you.' And then: 'Oh! I'm sorry. Awfully boring for you. It really isn't important. Let them live in their cesspool. They made it. It doesn't matter.'

She smiled and said simply:

'Are you supposed to caress my knee or break it in half?'

He laughed and put both hands on the wheel. He had not realized how physical, how tautened, his feelings were.

'I'm supposed to be caressing you.' A rush of excitement pricked up through his throat. He spoke softly: 'All of you. Is it possible?'

'We'll see,' she said.

In the house, in the westward sun, still warm enough to give her body exactly the smooth soft heat of a bird's egg, they lay for a long time on the little bed. Wood-pigeons, taking up from each other chains of unfinished notes, cooed drowsily from the cedar trees. A butterfly, sulphur yellow, floated leaf-like about the balcony.

During some part of this time he could not help thinking of Cordelia. This, perhaps, was the first, the perfect opportunity to break Cordelia's bridge-playing, impervious heart. Even Cordelia, perhaps, would not be able to bear, without some sort of action, love on the doorstep. Perhaps it was after all an excellent thing that Medhurst and his slut had seen the little ceremony of threading the orchid into his buttonhole: perhaps not a bad thing after all that in two days, even less, everyone would know of it, Cordelia included. Fitzgerald with a lady-friend in the village: even Cordelia, perhaps, would find it hard to put up with that. So out of it he would have loveliness and fun and then, by the summer's end, finish Cordelia too.

'I still can't understand why you don't open this house. It's so beautiful –'

'Economic impossibility.'

'What words. If it were mine I'd open it and damn the economics. Make the gardens nice again. Live in a little part of it –'

'And what are you doing now?'

She smiled, turning her body, her mouth swift in its teasing flicker:

'Loving in a little part of it.'

Her legs, long and golden-naked on the grey fire-watching blanket, were fuller and more lovely than he had, only the previous evening, imagined they would be. He touched them softly with his hands. He felt instantly a sharp quiver of response, fiery, almost painful, run up through her body and end in a convulsive hungry flick of her mouth against his own.

'Be careful how you do that,' she warned him. It was still with a little smile. 'You may be sorry –'

'Didn't I start it?' he said. 'Didn't I let you in with the key?'

'I've still got the key. But just be careful how you do that to me –'

In a long almost drowsy movement she stretched herself full length on the bed.

'What are you thinking of?' she said.

'Nothing –'

'Admiring me?'

'You're so lovely –'

'Nice man,' she said.

Outside, beyond the sun-bathed balcony, he could hear summer growing in the evening voices of drooning pigeons and in the throaty sweetness of several blackbirds in woods along the river. Bees were still working, perhaps on a tree of roses, just beyond the window, on the house wall. He could feel all summer growing and deepening in those sounds. He could feel it in the turn of her body, in the flame of butterfly wings darting yellow across the sun. He could even feel it in a curious softening and mounting ache in his own limbs. It was mounting and deepening and richening everywhere, rapidly and luxuriantly, with his own miles and miles of grass.

'I've a feeling the summer is going to be wonderful,' he said. 'Wonderful fun.'

'I think so too,' she said.

5

It did not strike him as curious, afterwards, whenever they met in the small room at the top of the empty house, sun-drenched and stifling as summer settled into weeks of heat, that she did not mention love.

It was certainly, people were saying, the most wonderful summer for years. This, they said, was what you called a summer. You knew, with such a summer, where you were. Day unfolded after day, hot and tranquil, settled under blue soft skies, into distances shortened and trembling under heat haze. In the garden a rapid luxuriance of nettle and thistle and yellow ragwort sprang up, with thickets of wild rose and frothy elder, to choke what had once been paths and beds and lawns between the crumbling walls. On the house the snow-broken magnolia lifted immense copper-green leaves centrally filled by buds of solid waxy cream. A pale bluish fire sprang from the tips of cedar branches. Across the park the great limes were early in flower and down across the meadows the hay was early too.

The girl did not speak of love; and perhaps, if he had noticed it, he would not have thought it extraordinary, since he did not speak of it either. But occasionally, as he waited for her in the wilderness of weeds and briar at the back of the house, and she was a little late, merely perhaps ten minutes or so, he experienced once again an uneasy stab of disappointment, a scratching edge of doubt that she would let him down. But that too did not trouble him again once she arrived.

All summer, continually, she spoke instead about the house. She would lie dreamily on the bed and reproach him in the gentlest terms about its emptiness. She would apply to it the word she never applied to him and which he, in turn, was not for some long time to apply to her.

'Oh! I love this house. I love it. I can't understand –' She did not tire, all summer, of the fabrication of that one particular dream: of how she would open the house, burn the briars, see the lawns once again smooth and short, the peacock trailing across fresh bright grass, the roses tied to the house-wall, the camellias given light and care. 'If you only opened it for the summer. A little of it. A room or two –'

'But good God,' he would say. 'It would cost a mint. Twenty or thirty thousand pounds.'

'Would it ruin you?'

'My dear child, I'm a business man.'

'Would it ruin you? Why do you want money?'

That, he told himself, was a question people often asked when they had none themselves. It always bored him to try to answer it.

'How much do you suppose you have?' she said. 'Altogether?'

'I wouldn't know.'

'Marvellous man,' she said. Her teasing had behind it, sometimes, a touch of shrewdness: exact rather than hard. 'First he doesn't know he has camellias in his garden. Then it's peacocks. Now it's money.'

'Well, I won't say I couldn't guess –'

'All right: guess,' she said.

'My father left a quarter of a million,' he said. 'I suppose if you count the farm and the stock and the house and the hop-business and so on there's probably the same again. Perhaps more.'

'It doesn't mean anything,' she said.

'No?'

His turn to be a little teasing now, he thought. Strange how people took that attitude; curious how they could feel that money, in great lumps, became negative.

Or was she probing? he thought. Trying to size the chances up? That, ten years ago, was what Cordelia had done. In his stupidity he had not seen it and now her teeth were in and he could not get them out.

Unexpectedly she said:

'It doesn't mean anything to me, I mean. What can you do with it every night? Look at it? You can't even count it.'

'Like a good old-fashioned miser,' he said. 'No. But I have it to look at. In things. In the land. In the grass.'

She smiled. It was already full summer, almost the middle of July, and the last of the hay, drying sweetly along the meadows, filled the air as it blew in through the balcony window with its delicious sun-ripe breath. Was there anything more wonderful than that?

'You and your grass,' she said. 'You're a grass god – that's what you are.'

'I've got fifteen hundred acres of it. That's true.'

'You've got everything.'

No: not everything, he thought. Not quite. He was struck by thoughts of Cordelia: ever-present, the leech, the bloodsucker who would not let go.

'Some things you can't buy,' he said.

'Oh! nonsense. You can buy anything. You know perfectly well.'

'Not the things Cordelia won't give.'

'Oh! damn Cordelia,' she said. 'Damn wives. Don't bore me with wives.'

'Wives are never so important as when they bore you –'

She sighed, stretching her body on the bed, giving a voluptuous twist of her long full legs, pressing herself down into it with the softness of a bird settling down on a nest.

'I don't want to be a wife,' she said. 'I'm free. I'm something you can have for nothing: for the fun of it –'

Something about the way she said this, casual and clipped and thrown away, went through his body like flame. In a flash, briefly extinguished, like a stab of heart-burn, it jolted him: steely and brutally sudden and withdrawn, leaving in its place a painful emptiness.

At the time he did not understand it. He was simply shaken by its unexpectedness. Almost immediately he felt he wanted to take her and hold her simply and quietly there where she lay. He pressed his mouth against her face. Out in the garden and beyond it there was hardly a sound of summer. The land had been drugged, almost stunned, by a week of continuous heat; the nightingales had finished singing and with them the cuckoos and almost every other bird but a few monotonous piping yellow hammers chipping away in the stifling heat of hay-filled afternoons. It was such wonderful weather, people said, marvellous weather indeed, perfect: magnificent for things like garden parties and games and flower shows. You felt so safe; you could plan things, as you so rarely could in England, weeks and weeks ahead.

She had been lying in the sun a good deal all summer, mostly half out on the balcony of the little room, so that now her body had taken on something of the colour of tawny-golden hay. They had come to an arrangement by which she had the key of the house too. In that way she could let herself in and wait for him.

And each time he wondered, as he climbed up through the deserted airless house, with its spidery sun-woven shabbiness, its army blisters and its scars of decay, whether she would be there: whether by some chance she would let him down.

And each time she was there; she did not let him down. Each time he climbed the stairs with a heart beating a little faster but without a conscious touch of anxiety. It was just something, the very faintest wonder, hardly even a doubt, as to whether she would be there, whether she would fail.

Earlier in the summer he had had the happy thought, one evening, of bringing up a picnic basket of drinks, a few bottles of champagne, and a box of biscuits. He was late coming down from town sometimes: business, a board meeting, an irritating slow-motion session with one of his men, who could not explain in twenty minutes what he himself could have explained in three, a session with Fawcett about estate matters, a train not on time. And on these occasions he had his doubts in reverse: not that she would not have arrived, but that she would have been, grown bored and have gone.

But that too never happened. She was always quite happy to lie there waiting: the champagne ready in one of the old fire-buckets but never opened; reading or asleep or half-asleep, her body growing deeper brown, a pure corn-colour, as July turned to August and the splendid dry heat carried on into September.

What was it she had called him? A grass god? Well, in a way it was true. In a way perhaps that explained him. But it was she, really, who was much more like a goddess. She was like the composite figure of all the long summer. She had been just so perfect and delicious, so changeless and dependable, and always so beautiful, ever since that lovely evening he had first met her when the oaks were breaking into flower and the nightingales were in song above the bluebells and both of them had agreed, quite truthfully as it turned out, that the summer would be fun.

But suddenly, for him, the summer was not fun.

6

He came back on a hot September afternoon from a day in London and drove round the estate, as he often did, before going home. It was so hot that he stopped and took off his city coat and hat as he drove the car across the park and through the lanes. September had come in with a lovely spell of high tranquil skies, blue and hot as July: so that everywhere people were saying that they could not remember such a summer. There were others who said it reminded them of another summer, when all the ponds had dried, or another summer, when there were corn-fires everywhere, or still another year when, even in England, cattle had to be killed for want of water. It seemed, they said, as if it would never end.

On the higher farms, where land was inclined to sandiness and there were stretches of pine-heath and bracken with birch-trees, he saw water-carts at work across the fields that day. The pine-heath developed, lower down, into a stretch of common land, rippled purple now with heather. The soil was a good six-foot depth of peat there. He had never been able to do anything with it; and that afternoon he saw that it was on fire.

As he stopped the car and got out to stand and look at it, one of his men came along the road, riding a bicycle. He stopped too and touched his cap.

'The peat's alight again, sir,' he said.

'Yes.'

'That'll burn like that for weeks, sir. No putting it out.'

'No.'

'I recollect '21, sir. It burned then. It burned half the summer. The fire keeps running underground.'

'That's the trouble,' he said.

'That is, sir. You think you got it out but you never have. It's always there. Burning down where you can't see it.'

He did not answer this time. Together he and his man watched for a moment or two longer the smoke trailing slowly across purple-brown islands of bracken and heather, blackened by veins of creeping flameless fire; and then the man got on his bicycle and rode away, calling back:

'That's goin' to be pretty serious soon, sir, if we don't get no rain.'

Presently, when he drove on, he found that it was really too hot, after a longish day in the city, to drive very far, and

he turned the car for home. The man was right; it was pretty
serious, he thought. Across the huge expanse of park and
field there was not a blade of green; his land was a series of
parched dust-brown chess squares encased by withering
hedges. Summer had driven with its own fire deep into grass
roots everywhere, giving pasture the look of being killed.
He knew, of course, that it was not killed; he knew grass
better than that. Grass was an amazingly eternal thing, quite
indestructible, and would come again, with a shower or
two, miraculously.

He drove home. Through tiredness, perhaps through the
exceptional heat, he felt irritated by the sound of voices
coming from the garden, over the high wall, as he put the
car away.

It was only as he began to go towards the house, carrying
his hat and coat over his arm, that he realized that the house,
the garden and even the former pigsty summer-house were
full of people. Fifty or sixty people were there: grinning,
talking, sucking at glasses. Too late he remembered his
wife's party.

'There you are!' people called to him. 'How was town?
Exhausting?'

He wandered into the garden with a glass of gin in his
hand. The lawn was full of a drinking, gaping, parrot-like
chorus. He could not see his pergolas of late fading roses for
a barricade of hats.

Out of it all came his wife, moving towards him with the
swift persistence of a blue silk leech. He moved to avoid her
but she came on, whispering between her teeth.

'Amazing how you always manage to forget.'

Frigidly, tired, he apologized: 'I had to call at the estate
office. I'm sorry.'

'Well for God's sake circulate now you're here.'

'I thought it was your party,' he said. 'Your friends.'

She gave him a curious fleeting malignant shadow of a
grin that he did not understand for some moments afterwards.

'Some of your friends are here too,' she said.

She moved away, holding her glass well above the line of

her face as she squirmed across the party-crushed lawn. It might have been a touch of triumph about something, but he was too tired to give it a second's further thought.

He wandered to where, at the end of the lawn, the first rose-purple michaelmas daisies drooped like tired feathers among bronzy gold and scarlet dahlias in the heat. The garden was going to pot, he thought, absolutely and completely to pot; and after people had called to him for the fifth or sixth time 'Hullo, Fitzgerald. How was town? Pretty grim I expect?' he decided his obligations were all fulfilled.

There was time to have one more drink before he got the car out and drove across the park to where, as always, the girl would be waiting.

But suddenly, out of the crowd of parrot-heads and hats and glasses, he saw her actually there, on the lawn, not thirty feet away, watching him.

He felt himself go cold, drained of reaction. He could not move. He could not even lift his glass to his mouth. For more than a minute he simply stood staring at her, stunned and cold and without thought.

She was wearing a dress of pale yellow with a narrow black belt and long black gloves. Yellow was her favourite colour. Now it seemed to make her look taller than ever. The waist of the dress was rather high, and her long beautiful legs seemed to give the whole of her body a wonderfully elegant and elevated slenderness. Nothing she could have worn, he thought, could have thrown her so much into relief against the crowd of gabbling sucking faces.

Recovering a little, he looked across the lawn and raised his glass to her. It seemed to him that she looked deliberately away.

For the second time he felt himself go cold. He was shot through by a ridiculous and paralysing thought that she was never going to speak to him again. Always, at the back of his mind, there had been the notion that somehow, one day, for perhaps the most trivial of reasons, she would let him down. Now it came back.

It was not until he had lifted his glass to her a second time and she had looked away again, avoiding him completely, that he felt the full bleak pain of it. She was there, but suddenly she did not want him. He felt himself turn sick. He looked at her again, and again she turned away. She was wearing a large lacy transparent hat that matched her dress. Black yellow-stamened flowers were clustered on one side of it and the soft brim came down and touched her shoulders. And finally and completely, as she turned her back, the hat shut him away.

He went back into the house, stopping to get himself another drink from a tray in the hall. Always, at parties, he felt himself to be a stranger in his own house. People like beetles crawled about the place, admiring glass and furniture, gabbling, shouting to make themselves heard.

'How does the drought affect you?' someone said, and he found himself in a corner with his local rector, a man with a face like a knobbed and polished club.

For some moments he exchanged absent-minded hopes and pleasantries about the prospect of rain.

'We are offering prayers,' the rector said.

'Are you?' he said.

He excused himself and went to get a third drink. Draining it down, he knew suddenly that he was being quite ridiculous, that he was behaving like a fool. It was perfectly obvious that she could not possibly speak to him there. Only an idiot could have failed to see that; or that she was behaving in the only possible and sensible way.

'Your wife has a genius for parties,' someone said. 'They are always terrific.'

With a stab of anger he remembered Cordelia. Malignant, leech-like, draining Cordelia. For the first time his mind was clear. Cordelia with the genius for parties, Cordelia with the nice notion of inviting the girl: stupid of him not to have seen that it was all Cordelia.

Out in the garden, as she passed him, Cordelia smiled. Its infuriating slightness seemed to propel him blindly to the far side of the lawn. He searched vainly for the yellow dress.

The party was thinning out a little and now people began to come to him and shake hands, to thank him and say good-bye.

'You must thank my wife,' he said. 'She's the genius who does these things.'

He walked beyond the pergola to where, in the vegetable patch, a few people were walking apart from the crowd. Here two tall prop-like maiden ladies poked with grey silk parasols at the cracked earth across which even weeds were blue and flaccid with drought.

'We do not understand the vegetables with the purple flowers,' they said to him. 'They are new to us.'

'Artichokes.'

'Oh! no, surely. They grow underground.'

'There are two kinds,' he said.

'How extraordinary, how interesting.'

Suddenly, from behind high half-withered rows of flowerless beans, he saw the flash of the yellow hat and dress.

'But does one eat them?' the ladies said.

'One eats the top.'

The girl, with the woman he took to be her sister, was coming up the path. He stared straight at her. His body was shot through with a single quivering start of pain as he saw the long slender legs moving under the yellow dress; he saw the taut full breasts, through the thin summery material, quivering slightly as she walked. He tried for a moment or two to fix the dark elongated eyes, but they did not look at him.

'How does one eat it?' the ladies asked. 'It is like a thistle.'

'One eats it at an earlier stage,' he said.

The girl, only four or five yards away, was looking straight ahead.

'Cooked?' the ladies said. 'One eats it cooked of course?'

'Like asparagus,' he said. 'With sauce.'

'Strange how one never comes across it.'

'It's eaten more in France,' he said.

As he spoke the girl came level with him and he stepped

aside to let her pass. He thought how extraordinarily beautiful she looked and he was moved by an intolerable impulse to touch her hand as she went by. For a moment it obliterated everything. He felt he had never wanted anything in his entire life quite so much as that. It filled him with a painful, blinding sort of hunger and there was nothing he could do.

'Well, thank you, Mr Fitzgerald,' the ladies said. 'It is Mr Fitzgerald, isn't it?'

'Yes.'

'We were not certain. We know your wife much better of course.'

He did not speak again. Wandering vaguely back into the crowd, across the lawn, he was aware simply, with dry and lacerating emptiness, that the girl had gone.

When the last car had driven away he walked upstairs to his room. It was dark and he felt he did not want a light. But as he came along the landing a door opened, a shaft of light pounced across the stairs, and he saw Cordelia waiting there in her dressing gown.

'Good night,' he said.

The house was hot and stale. Suddenly he did not want to be in it any longer. He turned to go downstairs.

'I must say she's very beautiful,' Cordelia said.

'Is there any need to talk about it?'

'I think we ought to talk about it.'

'I don't see why,' he said. 'I'm going down for a drink.'

As he reached the top of the stairs, Cordelia said:

'I want to talk about it. Now.'

'Oh?'

With astonishing and unexpected directness she said:

'The whole district is stiff with gossip. There has been dirty, evil, rotten gossip.'

'They're not happy unless they have a little gossip,' he said.

'Happy!' she said. 'It's nice the way you talk about happy.'

'I didn't want to talk at all,' he said.

He had not stopped walking down the stairs. Now, half-way down, he heard her scurrying after him, her voice bitterly running too in a series of leaf-like whispers:

'You might at least have the decency to stand still while I say something!'

'All right,' he said. He had reached the foot of the stairs. He could hear the two maids washing glasses in the kitchen. 'I'll stand still.'

'Not here,' she said. 'Not here.'

He unlocked the cellarette on the sideboard and found the whisky. With the decanter in one hand and a glass in the other he walked to the door.

Out in the narrow courtyard the scent of late summer, heavy and intoxicating with tobacco flowers, was so delicious that he walked for ten or fifteen yards, breathing fresh sweet air, before he realized she was following him.

'If you'd have the decency to stand still a minute I could say what I have to say.'

'I'm standing still.' He mocked her with an arresting flick of the decanter. 'One minute.'

'What I want to say won't take a minute,' she said.

'Good,' he said. 'Splendid.'

Always there was the same niggling, pointless, wearisome row after parties. He did not want to listen. There could be no point in listening. He remembered suddenly, for no reason at all, the old ladies who had not heard of artichokes. They were the sort of idiotic, suburban, boring people she knew.

It was so monstrously stupid that he began laughing.

'I don't think it's any time for laughing.'

'No? There were two ladies who had never heard of artichokes,' he said. 'Your friends. Damn funny.'

'Awfully funny.'

For a moment they were both tensely silent; and then she said:

'If the joke is over I want to talk about the cottage. The one at Sandchurch. By the sea.'

'Good God, why?'

'I'm going to live there,' she said. 'You're going to give it me.'

Vaguely, at last, he began to understand what it was she had wished to speak about. A few early stars were pricking the clear darkness across the park, above coast-like undulation of trees, and he watched them, fascinated, incredulous at what he heard.

'You always get what you want,' she said. 'You always have done. In time.'

He did not speak.

'That's the way you were brought up,' she said. 'All you had to do was to scream long enough and they gave it you.' She stopped and then went on: 'I don't think you're selfish. You're just not aware of other people.'

The tobacco-plants, pale and ghost-like under the wall of the house, were almost the only things that had survived, with any freshness, the long blistering heat of summer. He took a slow deep breath and held the sweetness of them in his mouth.

'Well, you've got this,' she said. 'You wanted it all summer and now you've got it.'

Her generosity seemed to call for some sort of remark, but he could think of nothing; and she said:

'All I want is the cottage and a little place and enough to live on.'

'I think that's more than fair.'

'I'm not trying to be fair,' she said. 'But you can't go on without love, can you? It's silly to go on without love.'

For a very long time, he thought, there had never been any question of love. That, above all, had never intruded.

'Once there's no love,' she said, 'it's the end.'

Well then, he thought, thank God there was no love. The stars over the dark line of trees were growing brighter every moment, flashing crystal green in the hot September sky. To the right of the big house, in the hollow, reflections of fire filled the darkness, and he remembered there were hop-pickers camping there. It was lovely weather for the hopping.

In a flat voice Cordelia said:

'I apologize about the party. The girl I mean. It was not vindictive.'

'No?'

'I didn't even know her name till this week. I didn't even believe she existed. I had to invite her to make sure.'

Well, that was decent, he thought. And really without rancour.

'I had to know her name, after all,' she said. 'I have to name her –'

For a moment it occurred to him that she was going to cry. He thought he heard her sniff in the darkness, but it might have been her shoe grating dry gravel as she turned to go. It did not strike him as curious that she did not say good night. But he said good night himself, and afterwards, as she walked away, thank you.

Later, for some time, he walked about the garden, deliciously breathing the deep scent of tobacco flowers. How wonderfully they had done all summer, he thought, how marvellously they had stood the drought where other things had failed. The sky was full of stars. An owl called with fluffy notes across the park. He walked up and down the garden, thinking. He thought of the girl, the yellow dress, her brown arms in the long black gloves, the little room, the long matchless summer and of how, at last, because of it, he was going to be free. Curious that his own key, in his own gate, in his own park, on that first evening, had begun it all.

When he went to bed he fancied he heard Cordelia crying in her room. But he was not sure; and he did not stop to see. Women cried for the oddest things – sometimes for pleasure; but mostly you never knew why.

7

When he drove across the park the following evening it was still very hot and the peat land fires were still smouldering, raising smoke that hung about in thin blue-brown clouds.

He had come up to the house a little earlier than usual, and when he reached the room in the top of the house the girl was not there. He felt suddenly more than worried. He felt once again the gnawing misery of the notion that she would let him down.

For a short time he sat on the bed, trying patiently to wait for her. It was unbearably hot in the little shut-up room and he found himself sweating. It was a sweat of anxiety, touched by fear and aggravated by sun; and after ten minutes or so he could not bear it any longer.

He went downstairs, through the empty airless house and out into the front courtyard of withered grass and weeds to look for her. He walked once round the house and stood looking vainly down the long avenue, past the ruined army huts and drifts of premature shrivelled chestnut leaves, dead and brown on the road.

'Sir?' a voice said. 'Excuse me, sir?'

He turned and, in a moment of sharp annoyance, saw Medhurst, touching his cap as he came from behind the army huts.

'What do you want?' he said. 'How did you know I was here?'

'I saw the car, sir.'

'What are you doing sneaking about the house here?'

'I wanted a word with you, sir,' Medhurst said. 'It was about the water.'

God, he thought, the water again. Always the water. He remembered with revulsion and annoyance the fetid hut, the naked unwashed baby. If you gave them water, Good God, they hadn't the faintest notion in hell what it was for.

'Well, what about the water? You made any use of it yet?'

'No, sir,' Medhurst said. 'We got none to use. We had none to use this three weeks.'

'You mean the well has packed up?'

'Dry as a bone, sir.'

'Then why the hell didn't you speak of it before? Why didn't you speak to Captain Fawcett?'

'I spoke to Captain Fawcett, sir. We been having water carted down there. It wasn't that, sir –'

'Then what are you cribbing about?' There was too much sir, too much lying and hedging, too much shiftiness. 'What are you driving at?'

'I can't stand another winter there, sir. We had a terrible winter and a terrible summer. The place is not fit for pigs, sir – '

He wanted to laugh; his voice broke in his throat, dryly. Impotent fury, another recollection of the ghastly unwashed hut, the little place that had been so pretty in his boyhood and was now nothing but a monstrous and sordid slum under the hazel trees: all of it clotted his tongue so that not a syllable of either laughter or fury or protest came.

'That's about as plain as I can put it, sir. I can't stand another winter –'

Where was the girl? he thought. For God's sake, where had she got to? He almost shouted:

'I've no time to go into this now. You must come down to the office. You must see me there.'

Grimly, scowling, and yet somehow smoothly and terribly polite, Medhurst said:

'I've worked for you and your father since I was thirteen –'

'Then very probably it's time you worked for someone else.'

'If that's the way you look at it, sir –'

'It is the way I look at it.' He was tired, impotently, wretchedly, miserably tired, and said: 'Good Christ, man, you can hear, I hope, can't you?'

'Yes, sir.'

Fitzgerald turned to walk away and saw at last, far down the avenue, under the chestnut trees, the girl walking towards him. A stab of excitement and gladness whipped through his throat and he was really not listening when Medhurst said:

'I want to get this straight, sir.'

'Straight?' he said. There was a new sort of insolence in the air nowadays; there was not one of them that wasn't at heart, he thought, a damn bolshevik. 'How do you mean straight?'

'You mean I'm to go, sir?'

'I do. You see Fawcett in the morning and Fawcett will fix you up.'

'You bloody well ought to be shot, sir,' Medhurst said. 'That's what you bloody well ought to be.'

Fitzgerald walked away. Nothing annoyed him more than passages of insolent and rowdy argument with disgruntled employees on the estate. He kept an agent for that. He walked on imperviously, as if indifferently; and at last, as he reached the stone steps of the house-front, he heard from Medhurst a cold low yell:

'You ought to be shot. And there's one or two as'd be glad to do it. Me, for one! –'

He did not turn or glance or utter a word in answer as he pushed open the door and went inside the house.

He was still standing there, just inside, in the deserted empty entrance hall, with its scarred and ruined panels, when the girl ran up the steps.

He felt now that he could hardly wait for her. As she swung open the door and came inside he pressed her back against it, kissing her mouth hard and for a long time. Hunger, a curious dry loneliness, an ache not at all unlike fear, held him rigid.

'I thought you were not coming. I had the most awful feeling –'

'Am I late? I've been busy. I tried not to be.'

He was bursting to tell of Cordelia, and said:

'Shall we go up?'

'I really mustn't stay long –'

'Not another party?' he said. Gladness that she had now arrived broke the small amusing irony about yesterday. 'Surely not a party?'

'Poor man,' she said, and laughed. 'The look on your face.' Her laugh was nothing more than a few light chuckles low in her throat. 'As if I were never going to speak to you again.'

'That's what I felt,' he said.

Upstairs, in the little room, she lay fully-dressed on the bed. He sat on the end of it, looking at her, his heart crowded with a new and extraordinary tenderness. He thought of her as she had looked at the party, in the yellow dress. There, in the garden, in the yellow dress, the long black gloves and the big hat that shut him away, she had woken in him these first startling, almost frightening impulses of new feeling. Queer that in that moment, held as it were behind a barrier set up by the two owl-like ladies talking of artichokes, in the moment when he could not touch her at all, he should have been first troubled by this uneasy, startling hunger of wanting her so much.

'I've something to tell you,' he said. What was it Cordelia had said about love? It was no use without love –

'Tell on,' she said.

Outside, in the long dead forest of grass, he fancied he heard the dry shufflings of the peacock: the wandering dainty ghost that had trailed about there behind the house all summer.

'Cordelia is going to let me go.'

The girl, staring upwards, seemed to be listening to the peacock too.

'It was really why she invited you,' he said.

'Why me?'

Her voice seemed to be echoed in the peacock's dry rustlings through dead grass.

'I think it was the yellow dress that did it,' he said. 'I think you scored quite a victory in the yellow dress.'

She did not answer. Her quietness was so strangely rapt and withdrawn and cool that it briefly occurred to him that she did not think there had, in fact, been any victory.

He lay down beside her on the bed.

'Say something, please. Say something,' he said.

On evenings in May and June, when they had first come there, the clamorous chorus of birds and warm late evenings, just before darkness, and even after darkness, had been wonderful. Now summer had killed all bird-sound except the delicate stalking of the peacock: an irritating haunting sort of a whisper in the ruined garden, in a world that was like an old and dusty vacuum.

'I love you: that's what,' he said. 'Don't you know?' Tenderly he tried to turn her face to him and found it withdrawn and rigid. 'Don't you know? You love me too, don't you?'

'No.'

He felt himself savagely hit between the eyes as if by a black and sickening flash of flame.

'God – ' As he began to speak he hardly heard her, in turn, talking quietly, almost as if to herself, as she stared through the balcony window at the hot September sky:

'It's why I was late to-night. I've been packing.'

'Packing? – for God's sake?'

'I'm going on Wednesday,' she said. 'The day after to-morrow.'

He sucked dry dusty air through his mouth, ejecting it again in odd dead words:

'But all summer' – stupidly and incoherently he searched for words of argument – 'after all that's happened – the things we've done.'

'You never mentioned love,' she said. 'You never talked about it.'

'But how can you say? It's a thing that gets hold of you. It gets down inside you. You can't say what you want it to be. How can you say?'

'You wanted it to be fun,' she said. 'That's what you said.'

Suddenly, bitterly hurt, he had nothing to say. He was crushed by a dark complexity of emotions. He was not used to such complexity. His body was held rigid, in bloodless paralysis, and outside in the garden the damnable, infuriating rustle of the peacock was the only sound that broke the air.

'I ought to go,' she said.

She moved as if to get up; but in an unbearable impulse to touch her, to hold her down there on the bed, he ran his hands across her neck and breasts, and she said:

'I warned you what it might be. I warned you long ago.'

A terrible and dull soreness, like a bruise, seemed to drag downward across his chest.

'It's been wonderful and I've loved the house,' she said. 'I've loved everything. But everything comes to an end. I loved everything but it has to come to an end.'

He felt beaten about by emotions that were so baffling and complex that they made him feel ridiculous. It was cruelly stupid that in agony a man could feel ridiculous.

'Let me get up now,' she said. She moved her long body quietly away from him on the bed.

'May I kiss you?'

'You know you may.' She was suddenly cool and withdrawn and shut away, as she had been that first evening he had brought her there: the evening she had called him 'Careless man' as he clumsily broke the camellia flowers.

He kissed her for the last time. He wanted the kiss to flame against her mouth with the love he could not express in words; but her mouth in its responses was dry and cool, and the kiss was dry too, utterly removed from the molten complicated agony that raged inside him. He wanted to break away from the long supple body, exquisite more than ever now, always so beautiful and so obliging and so like summer, and let the agony release itself in a scream telling her that he could not bear it and that she did not understand.

Instead it was she who broke away. Sitting up, she ruffled her brown hair with her hands – with pain he loved its cat-like fluffiness, all shining and free, as it fell and rose with the toss of her head – and then swung her legs to the floor.

'It's all over,' she said. 'I'm sorry.' She touched his face with her hand. 'The summer's over.' One of her fingers seemed to draw a mask across his cheek. 'It was fun,' she said. 'Like you said it would be –'

He heard her go downstairs, her footsteps hitting emptily on the hollow treads, echoing emptily through the deserted house.

Then suddenly he heard her running back. A flash of triumph went through him. After all, he thought, she could not bear it without him; there was going to be one of those moments of reconciliation; she was coming back – he stood waiting, tensely, as he watched the swing of the opening door.

'Only the key,' she said. 'I forgot the key. You'll need it again some day –'

He left it where she let it fall on the bed. Sharply and painfully it made him remember the evening he had first given it her: the exquisite May evening of cuckoo sounds, of nightingales, among the oak flowers and all the warm sap of spring; and then the next evening, when she had found the camellia flowers and had wanted so much to see the house and had taunted and teased him because of his folly in not opening it, in leaving it all to emptiness and decay.

And frantically he said:

'Wait a minute. Darling, don't go for a minute. Darling, I've got something to say.'

'Well?'

'Listen,' he said. 'Don't go. Sit down a moment –'

She did not sit down. He made an imploring tremulous effort to draw her down to the bed, but the old dry coldness of his fear paralysed him again when he found she did not move.

'Listen – let's talk rationally.' He had never felt less like talking rationally in his life. He felt his teeth jar together, at the back of his dry mouth, making in his head a sound like the chattering of cold steel keys.

'Look,' he said, 'what would you say if I opened the house? You always wanted me to open the house.'

'Did I?'

'You always loved it – you always wanted it open. I could do it,' he said. 'I could open it for you –'

'You'll never open it,' she said.

'Oh! please,' he said. 'Darling. I'd like to open it. I'd like to do it for you – open it up, open the gardens, make everything as it was –'

'You'll never open it,' she said.

He sat on the bed, making a useless and unconvincing gesture of pain with his two hands, flinging them up and pressing them against his head. Then as they fell again he let them remain against her body, frontally, on the long smooth thighs. The rigid smoothness of her body, lovely and too familiar, made no sort of movement of relaxation.

'Let me open the house for you. Let me do that,' he said. 'That's what you always wanted.'

He looked up and saw her face, charming and maddening, friendly and tender, and yet distant as ever, and he knew that it was not something she had always wanted. He knew there was nothing of him she wanted. There was nothing of him she craved: neither himself, nor the house, nor even the little attendant charms she had loved as they came and went away: the camellias, the magnolias on the house wall – What was it Cordelia had said? If there was anything he wanted – something like that – he had simply to scream long enough and they gave it to him. He did not want to scream now, but suddenly he felt that he would have given anything, the house, the land, the grass, anything, in return for some simple gesture of hers, a word, the tiniest touch of friendliness, the merest indication that there was, after all, something of him that she wanted back. Was it so much to ask? he thought.

Instead he was aware only of the rigid unaltered position of her body, his own dry hard loneliness, and then her voice, saying again:

'You'll never open it. It's like opening a tomb. There's only the dead inside it. Whatever there was is dead and gone – it's finished, all this, it's the end.'

She moved away; the fine smooth thighs slipped out of his hands. He was tortured once again by blinding moments of futile agony combined with the renewed sensation of feeling ridiculous as he tried to clutch her body and bring it back. He began to say something about 'Darling, you can't go out like this, just like this – you can't end it like this,' and then she combed her fingers through her loose brown hair and tossed it back from her face and looked down at him sitting there, imploring and agonized, on the bed.

'One of us had to end it,' she said.

He could not look at her; the tips of his fingers were without feeling as he brought them together, hopelessly, where he sat, staring down.

'It's all dead,' she said. 'In your heart you know perfectly well it's dead.'

He heard her walk away. This time he made no attempt to stop her. After what seemed a long time a breath of wind caught the balcony window and rocked it backwards and forwards against the mullion. He got up and walked across to shut it, his hands trembling so much that the shutters chattered as he pulled them together. The sun was going down fierily, at eye-level, through a gap in the cedar trees, and for some moments, caught by the flash of it, he could not see.

Half blindly he went downstairs and then, in one of his moments of forgetfulness, not thinking of the car, he began to walk across the park.

He walked for some distance before he saw Pritchard, driving the big auger into drought-baked earth with his customary furious energy, bare to the waist now, his face and body pouring with sweat.

'You're a maniac with that thing,' he said.

'Yes: I suppose I am a bit of a maniac, sir.' Pritchard laughed. 'Just a bit –'

Fitzgerald stared at the daemoniac driving auger stabbing down into burnt dead grass.

'Not finding the water now?' he said. He laughed himself, crookedly.

'Oh! yes,' Pritchard said. 'Still here. Still signs of it. It's here all right – everywhere. '

Everywhere the summer had bitten deep, almost cruelly, into earth and grass, and only a spark was needed to fire, in a flash, acres of lifeless, colourless grass and shrivelled miles of woodland.

'Oh! yes,' Pritchard said. 'The water's here. It takes more than this –'

'Any good here for the cherries I spoke about?'

'Fatal. The soil's right, the situation is right – but the water –'

'Good God, man,' he said, 'you can't be serious about the water?'

'Dead serious,' Pritchard said. 'You see on land like this it isn't the drought that kills.' He crumbled with his fingers a few grains of waterless rust-brown earth and let them fall away in a little dusty cloud. 'It's the year after. Or the year after that. That's the one that kills.'

Fitzgerald, not answering, walked on across the park. Over on the heathland peat fires were burning more and more smokily, running underground where you could not put them out. All down the little valley there hung low blue-brown clouds from the fires and all across his land there was no longer a trace of the green of early summer he had loved so much, about the time of oak-flowers and the voice of the nightingale, and everywhere the grass was dead.

THE DELICATE NATURE

CAPTAIN CUSTANCE, standing on the bridge of the coaster *Roselay* as she swung in from seaward to enter the river mouth through what seemed to be two walls of excavated carmine mud decorated by fantastic clumps of grey sea-skinned tree roots, remarked in a brittle Newcastle accent that 'in a couple of minutes she would be grinding and grunting like a bloody factory.'

The swing of the *Roselay* to seaward had taken her wide and at right angles to a brilliant green and carmine barrier of coast; and now, as Captain Custance called down the engine tube for full ahead, she seemed to leap forward in a clumsy and shuddering charge, thrashing into the curdling sand-brown current of disgorging stream. And in two minutes, as Captain Custance said, she was grinding up between the walls of forest roots like a long lump of floating factory. Below there was a guttural wrenching of all her moving parts and above, from a high iron smoke stack, a long curling flag of cloud that melted sulphur bronze against the sun. Through her decks Simpson could feel her convulsive thunder on the soles of his feet, as if somewhere below him giant presses were hammering out continuous patterns through two-inch steel.

'You'll be there in three hours,' Captain Custance said. 'And this is' – he pointed to the shores – 'about all you'll see – this forest stuff – until you get there.' The high old-fashioned bridge seemed to pitch forward, like a crazy cage, suspending itself out over the bows of the *Roselay* as she cut through rich brown waters. 'The river's high this week. More muck than ever coming down.'

The face of Captain Custance had been coloured a mixture of bright yellow and bark-like brown by tropical sun, and it reminded Simpson, in its cross pattern of cracks and fissures, of a battered pineapple.

'Not here during the war, you said?'

'No.'

'Well: the country's changed a lot. A lot to be done. When did you say the great Malan was back?'

'In three weeks. Probably a month,' Simpson said.

'That'll give you time to settle down,' Captain Custance said. 'It used to be a fine estate up there. Rubber and pineapple. Then they went mad to grub every pineapple in the peninsula and plant rubber. And then rubber went down until it wasn't worth a dog's hair. And then the war. I dare say it's a bit rough up there with one thing and another – but it'll come back. I'm glad they're opening it up.'

Captain Custance, inspired perhaps by the presence of an only passenger, hardly ever closed his mouth. Even when not speaking he could not keep his lips still. He addressed the river before him with a series of preparations for spitting that never quite came off. Spittle seemed to be chewed into a ball and sucked about, from side to side, between the cadaverous fissures of his cheeks, to be finally and swiftly rolled forward, in a solid plug, behind his incongruously correct and scrupulous false teeth. At the moment when the ball of spittle seemed about to find access to the bows of the *Roselay* Captain Custance always thought of something fresh to say, and the spittle, hastily sucked back, was swallowed hard away.

'So you don't know the great Malan?'

Under the double wall of forest the air was clotted and terribly humid, paralysing, withering after the clearer heat of open sea. Sometimes, ahead, at a deeper bend of the stream, Simpson could see the flooding waters cut in at an angle against the brilliant forest banks, raising the smallest surface clouds of spray. It gave the impression, from that distance, seen against shadow, that the river was steaming under heat and sun.

It was now hardly necessary for Simpson to think of an answer to any questions about the great Malan. Sooner or

later Captain Custance would answer them for him. He
was anxious too, as he had been anxious down in Singapore
during three days of waiting there, not to put a foot wrong,
not to do anything to jeopardize his chances. Already Malan
had the beginnings of legendary shape about him. That was
bad enough. But what he wanted to avoid as much as that,
if not more, was to give away any suggestion that would
determine the shape of himself. It was too early; he was
very keen, perhaps too keen, to make an impression; he was
young and raw and he felt, as he talked to Captain Custance, very green.

'He's an old hand,' Captain Custance said. 'Well, I say
old – you know the way I mean. Old in the game is what I
mean. Came out young before the war. Went back when it
started. I suppose he wouldn't be older than you when I
brought him up here for the first time and I brought him a
time or two after that. Probably about forty now.'

A small brass bell, rung from the top of the companion-
way by the brown hand of a Malay, called Simpson, down
a moment later, the only passenger, to a lunch of what
turned out to be greasy chicken, surrounded by brown rice,
in the quaking, shuddering stifling confinement of the little
saloon.

Captain Custance called after him to be excused. You
never knew what muck there might be coming down. The
trip before last there had been a floating tree as big as a
church steeple that had nearly done his bows in.

'Have a sleep down there in my bunk,' he called. 'The
boy will show you where it is. There's nothing to see up here
– not a bloody thing till I land you.' The flattened pineapple appearance of the face was heightened, as Simpson
saw it, from the deck below. 'I got a picture of the great
Malan I'll show you too – if I can rake it up.'

After the chicken and a slice or two of pineapple, un-
sugared, cut thinly, fresh and delicious, Simpson was glad
to lie down. In the captain's bunk he stripped down to his
shirt and lay in a stupefying sweat, listening to the throbbing shudders of the *Roselay* climbing against the stream. A

few voices called high pitched conversation during the afternoon, fighting the clamour of the floating factory. He tried to sleep, but some time later a Malay steward brought him a cup of scalding coffee, waking him from a doze. He drank the coffee, when it cooled, purely for thirst's sake and then lay thinking, suddenly lonely, of Singapore. There had been two very nice fellows, Ford and Harrison, men of his own age, in Singapore. They had looked after him; there had been much banter and drinking of farewells. For three days and nights they had gone out of their way to be nice to him, stinting nothing, giving him little tips on this and that, talking with airy reassurance of the up-river station, telling him what a simple, sweet assignment, for a new man, it was. They had agreed, over and over again, what a marvellously lucky fellow he was – 'nobody to worry you, old boy. Your own boss. Back here in a month – six weeks at the outside. All you've got to do is wait for Malan.'

They were very nice fellows; he would miss them very much. He felt loneliness, dry and vacant, consume the pleasant recollections. Even under gin he had omitted to disclose to those two nice fellows that he had not the vaguest idea what a rubber tree looked like; or whether a pineapple grew, like coconuts, on a tree, or simply by the grace of God.

He slept a little after that, in a sweating, shuddering drowse, and Captain Custance woke him about four o'clock.

'I'll be putting you down in ten minutes,' he said. 'One of the boys'll get your kit. You think you got everything you need?'

'I think so.'

'Got chlorodyne? You'll need chlorodyne if your guts go wrong.'

'No.'

'You'd better have chlorodyne. I'll give you some from the chest. And if you need anything bringing up remember I'll be coming down-river Thursday about midday, and up again the Monday after.'

Captain Custance went on deck and Simpson dressed and followed him. He stood for a moment or two dazzled and drugged by a clash of white sunlight that descended with the stunning flatness of a board.

Then he walked up to join Captain Custance on the bridge and from there, poised on the quaking high-suspended cage, he caught his first sight of the Company's landing-stage, the waterfront. It seemed to consist simply of the timber of three packing cases nailed above a dozen jetty piles reinforced by a chain of cracking motor tyres.

Captain Custance, calling down the tube for slow ahead, did not seem to be interested in the desolation of this small deserted quay with its leaden glare of corrugated roofs. Simpson – he discovered later that these squares of glinting wreckage had been, and were still now called, the offices – could only stare.

'Nobody about,' Captain Custance said. 'There ought to be a boy or two. Need waking up.' He yelled down the speaking tube. From the funnel, in answer, came three blasts, short, sizzling, and booming, of the *Roselay*'s whistle. Sound and echo and sound and re-echo chased each other over forest and river in queer bloated jumps, uncanny and hollow, but from the jetty there was no movement or sound at all in answer.

'The bungalow's back there,' Captain Custance said. He pointed to vague recessions of reddish dust – once, Simpson later discovered, the main central road of the whole estate – penetrating the final corner of forest. 'Used to be there. I stopped off a time or two with the great Malan to have a drink.'

The landing-stage remained deserted. A glare of corrugated roofs, through one of which a tree had grown up and turned back a triangle of iron as neat as a segment cut from a pie, flashed back to Captain Custance and Simpson all the answer they were to get from another blast on the whistle. Some seconds later the *Roselay* hit the rubber tyres, bouncing back, churning to rest, and in that moment Captain Custance remembered the photograph of Malan.

'He left it in the cabin one day – always meant to give it back to him. Then the war came.' He held the picture out to Simpson, yelling incomprehensibly to the Malay crew letting down the gangway and forcibly reminding Simpson at the same time that he himself did not know a word of Malay, and then suddenly the engines stopped and with them, at last, all the thunderous quaking of decks that had convulsed and rattled the soles of Simpson's feet for the last four hours.

In that queer stillness and silence he was so surprised to find himself immobile at last, instead of jigging like an imbecile, that he forgot the photograph.

Captain Custance's stubby forefinger, pointing, reminded him of it and he looked down.

'That was soon after he first came out. In 'thirty-five.'

Simpson stared vaguely at a picture, the background for which seemed to be an English suburban back-garden with a swing on a tree, of a young man in riding breeches – a tall, robust, angular man with a girl in a tennis frock at his side.

'That's the girl he was going to bring out,' Captain Custance said. 'But it never came off. Too delicate or something. Don't look above seventeen or eighteen there, does she? He told me once she'd never stand the climate. Not with her delicate nature.'

Simpson stared away from the photograph to where, on the deserted jetty, the Malay boys were piling his bags, his bed-roll, and his rifle case in a careless heap like junk; and he suddenly yelled:

'Hi! Be careful with that rifle! Don't sling it about like that –'

The boys took not the slightest notice and Captain Custance lifted his brittle Newcastle voice to shout in Malay. A pretence of piling Simpson's bags more neatly followed at once, and Captain Custance said:

'You better begin to learn Malay. It's easy enough. No grammar to bother with. Just phrases – you'll pick it up like steam-o –'

Uncomfortably Simpson remembered the Malay-English

phrase book, bought in a Singapore bazaar, with which he hoped to conquer everything, and at the same time he handed back the photograph to Captain Custance.

'No, keep it,' the Captain said. 'No good to me. You can give it back to Malan. He's probably had fifty like her since then if I know him. She looks a bit delicate, don't she? The funny thing is the climate isn't bad. Same all the year round, more or less – it isn't bad. Keep the photo anyway.'

'Thanks,' Simpson said. 'Well, I'd better say good-bye.'

'Good-bye, young fellow,' Captain Custance said. 'Give the picture with my best compliments to the great Malan.' He broadened the crusty ridges of his yellow-brown face into a taut smile. 'Interesting to see what he says.'

'All right.' Simpson shook hands, suddenly liking the broad garrulous Custance far too much, not wanting to go. 'I might see you as you go back.'

'I'll toot you on the whistle,' the Captain said. 'And if you want anything be here – Thursday midday. Not lonely, are you?' Captain Custance winked heavily. 'Ought to look out for a nice little Chinese skirt. Pretty as little bantams. Stick to you like burrs off a hedgerow.'

Simpson, suddenly more lonely than ever, could not speak. As he went down the gangway and stood beside his baggage on the landing-stage he told himself that he would not turn, at any rate until the last, least painful moment, to wave good-bye, but the scream of the *Roselay*'s whistle startled him violently and before he could prevent it he was staring up at the receding ship, already churning fast away from the jetty like a flat smoking factory, with Captain Custance beaming fierily, an unbearably friendly figure in white cap and ducks, caught like a flapping bird on the high cage-like bridge as he waved good-bye.

He picked up his rifle case and slung it over his shoulder and walked up what had once been the road, leaving his baggage on the quay. A horrible thrust of nausea, sharp, almost caustic, a sensation of being alone on the edge of a continent, penetrated violently his whole body, seeming to drain the blood away. He heard a final blast from the

Roselay's whistle exploring – as if it were really for him, to make sure that there was no kind of barrier to stop the cut of sound and echo and re-echo in the surrounding infinite emptiness – the roof of forest on either side of the river, losing itself finally in the blue-dusty line of hills.

The silence afterwards brought on him something worse than a mere nausea of loneliness. Successive waves of panic, a conviction that there really was no one there among the deserted office shacks, not even a bandit – no bandits within a hundred miles, old boy, no trouble at all, Ford and Harrison had told him, you're lucky there, old boy – made him suddenly want to dash back, as if ghost-driven, to the friendliness of his own baggage on the quay. Dismally, at the same moment, he remembered that Captain Custance had forgotten the chlorodyne.

Abruptly all these sensations were dispelled by the appearance, up the road, of a turbaned, bearded figure bringing with it its own hasty cloud of dust.

It raced towards him on a bicycle.

As it alighted he had sense enough to see that it was almost as remote from a Malay as he was himself. Two big black Sikh eyes, a genial barbaric flashed Sikh smile from between beard and moustaches, a sort of happily brandished gesture of both hands as they slung the bicycle into the dust – every suspicion of foreignness was confirmed a moment later by a flood of speech in what, he thought, were three languages.

English was not among them. It was lucky, he thought, that a combination of geniality and barbarism in the Sikh temperament understood the importance of a smile. The black facial bear-skin broke into repeated arcs of delighted, almost merry whiteness. Overcome too, he shook hands, and the Sikh saluted.

'English, English?' Simpson said. 'You speak English?'
'No, no, no.'
'Good God. Nothing? No English?'
'No, no, no –' and with it the smiling half-shake, half-nod that could, as he discovered afterwards, mean anything.

He held down his despair. For another second or two the Sikh, taller than himself by some inches, stood grinning down. Simpson went through a few pantomimic, rather exaggerated gestures of washing his hands. The Sikh understood them and broke into cries, pointing down the road.

A few minutes later Simpson was at the bungalow. It was actually, he saw with delight, of brick, with the framework of windows and doors in teak and a roof at least of sun-proof palm. There was a long, shaded veranda, piled up now with neglected and punctured sacks of fertilizer put there under cover from rain.

As the Sikh showed him all this with pride, unlocking the door with a little ceremonious fling of his hands, the fertilizer stank, stale and low and insistent, in the heat of the afternoon.

'Sahib, Sahib, Sahib,' the Sikh kept saying, bowing repeatedly; and Simpson walked into the bungalow, into a shrouded world of teak and wicker and wooden chests, the rattan blinds down against the sun. Familiar though it was, almost too precisely in colonial key, it struck him with an effect of amazing unreality. There was even an English fireplace, built of brick, with mantelpiece of fumed oak colour, the bricks reddled scrupulously, and down on the hearth, like a strayed wedding present, one of those sets of glinting oxidized accoutrements for brushing up dust and cinders. He wondered if Malan had built it: if perhaps this masterpiece, this piece of provincial monumental, were a key to Malan. He wandered about, opening doors, peering about him and returning always to the Sikh, who watched him with delight and friendly pride.

'Wash?' he said at last, 'wash?' and again made the pantomimic exaggerated gesture with his hands.

When the Sikh took him through the kitchen it began gradually to appear that Malan had had something of a genius for creating comfort for himself. A shower, operated by ingenious treadle devices from outside, worked excellently, he afterwards found, over the cool concrete slab of bath floor. The Sikh brought him towels and he washed his hands. In the kitchen there were devices, looking like old-fashioned boot cleaners, for dusting shoes. Neat racks kept a great paraphernalia of crockery and cutlery in rigid order. A piece of beautiful ingenuity, in the sitting-room, made it unnecessary for anyone sitting down some distance from the window to go through the tiresome necessity of getting up in order to pull the rattan blind. By an arrangement of cords, clever, but not at all complicated, the sitter could work the blind. 'Malan?' he said. 'Malan Sahib?' and the Sikh bowed with unexpected gravity, without a smile.

There was one other room. The company had put it down, originally, as a billiard-room: a solacing piece of civilization for men cut off from gaieties in Singapore.

The Sikh let up the rattan blind. Light revealed the billiard-table to be still there: but covered now, Simpson saw, with boarding. And there, on the boarding, laid out with an efficiency almost terrifying, almost beautiful, a model railway.

He stood looking at it: a pattern of complicated steel, of elliptical crossing-veins, of bridges and signalling systems, trucks and sidings, gradients and stations, crack expresses. An infinite number of gadgets, he discovered later, were concealed about it like tricks. It was governed, always, without fail, by an astonishing, maddening fluency.

When he saw that it worked by electricity he put his finger on the switch. Nothing happened; and the Sikh cried his one word of English, 'No, no, no,' high-pitched, almost mocking, pointing to the dead arc light above the billiard-table, shaking his head.

Next morning, just beyond the veranda, Simpson found the inevitable generator that would give light to the house and power to the magnificent Malan-made toy. Meanwhile he was to exist, apparently, by oil lamps. He took a last incredulous look at the Malan-made world of trucks and and sidings, and grinning, said to the Sikh:

'Malan?' And then the natural unthinking echo of Captain Custance: 'The great Malan?'

In return, once again, the Sikh had nothing to offer, even in mockery, by way of a smile.

That night, just before rolling over to sleep, while the small oil lamp was still alight at his bedside, he remembered the photograph of Malan and the girl. He sat up for some time under the mosquito net, looking at it. The girl, in her white tennis frock, with her dark eyes set with engaging and minute precision at the camera, her pretty dark hair and her delicate nature – she had a slender and almost ephemeral fragility, he thought, not sick, but so very young and so physically light and strange – attracted him at once much more than Malan. He thought Malan looked, in the conventional riding breeches and checkered cap and waist-coat, like a dummy snugly stuffed with the straw of a terrible ordinariness. He sported what seemed to Simpson to be an impossibly curled moustache. A feeling of airy and intolerable pride – whether for himself or for the girl Simpson could not tell – flooded the entire picture.

Simpson gazed at it a little longer, wondering what sort of woman Malan was going to bring out with him this time. What was it that Captain Custance had said? – forty or fifty of them since this one? In the excitement and exhaustion and the momentary loneliness of the trip up the river he had forgotten that Malan had gone home, to England, for that special purpose. Within a month he would be bringing Mrs Malan back with him.

And Simpson, going to sleep with a jumble of crossing impressions that included the model train, the girl in the tennis frock and the taste of pineapple in Captain Custance's appalling little saloon, decided that to give the photograph back to Malan would not, after all, be the tactful thing.

At least, not yet.

Next morning the Sikh – he thought it would be much easier and more friendly to call him George – served him the first half of many pineapples, succeeded by several small fried eggs, for breakfast. It was ripe and delicious, without a tang of that sharp and wasping acid you experienced with pineapples at home, and he enjoyed it so much that he ordered the other half.

After breakfast he and the Sikh toured what was left of the estate on bicycles. An exquisite early morning, blue and powdery, gave way to a stunning heat. The bicycle on which he rode belonged, inevitably, to Malan. It was fitted with a number of neat and silvery gadgets which included a barometer and, strangely, a mirror in which traffic, if there had been any, could be seen approaching from behind. He felt he would not have been at all surprised if a radio had been concealed in the handlebars or a refrigerating device under the saddle. There was in fact a special receptacle, with tube, from which you could drink thermos-cooled water as you rode along, without the disagreeable business of alighting.

In due course it would be the job of Malan, with himself as assistant, to destroy every pineapple in the place and restore the estate to rubber. Already, on the wall of the bungalow sitting-room – in the so-called offices, by the quay, the Sikh was still keeping chickens – Malan's map of the new estate, all pink and green and blue, correctly and admirably contoured, a gem of neatness, was hanging for him to see. It struck him several times that Malan might have hung it there quite purposely, so that the young and uninitiated assistant should have no doubt, on arrival, where his duties lay.

Meanwhile the Sikh and himself, single-handed, quite alone on the actual estate except for the chickens, flocks of predatory paroquets that came to raid the Sikh's admirably irrigated little kitchen garden and some snipe that Simpson shot most days before breakfast, had nothing to do. Simpson reflected that he could not even amuse himself, even if he had wanted to, with the railway train.

He decided, instead, to learn Malay.

With his phrase book on the table between them, he faced the Sikh for several hours a day. Youthful and dogged, he would repeat from the phrase book, as best he could, one of those sentences of dialogue intended for the guidance of passing travellers:

'Have you any idea where I can find a post-office? What time is it? Could I have the bill for my room?'

In this way, question by question, answer by answer, simply by having nothing to do from six in the morning until darkness fell with a scarcely perceptible breath of coolness from the river, he learned Malay.

The following Thursday he heard the toot of the *Roselay*'s whistle coming up the river and he went down to talk with Captain Custance on the quay.

Captain Custance, more voluble than ever, came down to the landing-stage with several letters: three for Simpson himself, the others for Malan.

'Forgot the chlorodyne,' Captain Custance said. 'How's your guts? All right? I'll bring it up next time – you'll need it if your guts go wrong. There's nothing better if your guts go wrong. How's your Malay? Coming on? Getting it going?' He rattled off several exploratory phrases, keen and garrulous with delight that Simpson could reply. 'Brushing up your billiards? They tell me there's a damn nice table there. I got half a mind to push her a bit harder downstream next Sunday and stop for an hour and have a drink and play you for a bob.'

'The table's covered with a railway.'

'Covered? Covered with what?'

As Simpson explained Captain Custance manipulated stringy clots of spittle between rubbery and astonished jaws and finally ejected a long swift arrow to the quay.

'I got to see that,' he said. 'Christ Jesus that's something I got to see.'

'Bring your prayer book,' Simpson said.

'Bring what?' Obtuse astonishment put grey film on Captain Custance's eyes and irony was lost on him.

'Stay to lunch,' Simpson said. 'I'll get the drinks as cold as I can and George can do a curry.'

Captain Custance was so astonished, in a groping and

139

simple kind of way, that he did not even ask who George could be.

Of Simpson's letters two were from Ford and Harrison. Friendly as ever, hearty and with a certain charm, they recalled for him evenings in Singapore and hoped he would soon return. The other was from the Company. It too was friendly, in a formal way, and requested him 'to explore, as soon as is convenient to your good self, the question of local labour. Preliminary inquiries only at this stage, as to numbers available, are required, and no question of remuneration should be discussed, or suggested, at the present stage. Our Mr Malan will deal with such problems as may arise in that field on his immediate return.'

He rode off next day, with the Sikh, along roads of bludgeoning and dusty heat to the nearest village, four miles away. His taste for pineapples had declined. Even so he was glad, once on the outward journey and once as they returned, to stop and get the Sikh to slash open for him one of the fruits he could not destroy. Simpson sucked at it with dazed greed, washing the dust from his face at the same time.

At the village – he judged it to have, perhaps, three hundred people, housed variously in small palm huts, under bamboo stilts supporting sheets of corrugated iron and in square compounds of palm frond – the question of assessing local labour was not difficult.

There was no local labour to assess.

But a curious thing happened. He was pushing the bicycle along an open track dividing two rows of palm huts that had something of the look of a collection of crouching ant-hills when a figure ran down from one of them to meet him, laughing and holding out her arms.

She was one of the little Chinese women, pretty as bantams, delicate-eyed, slender arms branching beautifully from a simple frock of sleeveless shantung, of whom Captain Custance had spoken. As she came running down first one and then the other of her heel-less straw slippers fell off. In her excited joy she did not notice them and they lay behind her in the dust, looking like two tongues of scarlet, the silk of their bright linings gleaming as if polished by the rubbing of her feet. Without them she ran springingly, the side slit of her skirt dividing as far as her thigh, and from twenty or thirty feet away he saw her mouth open in a flutter of laughter, tumbling and delighted as she called something to him over and over again.

'O! Ka-Kăsih' it sounded like, 'O! Ka-Kăsih,' the word so much part of her laughter that he could not relate it to anything the Sikh had taught. 'Ka-Kăsih –'

And then, ten feet away from him, she stopped. He saw her look from the bicycle to his face, and then from himself back to the bicycle. She put both hands to her face, stopping her mouth, and then let the fingers run upward into her black hair like rigid ivory curls. She gave a little blubber of frightened astonishment and then looked from his face to the bicycle, shocked almost to despair, for the last time.

A moment later she turned and began to run. She darted back towards the house, as if remembering the slippers. A stunning yell came at the same moment from one of the huts, and she doubled round, floundering and swift, exactly like a tiny scuttling hen, dipping and darting between hedges of creeper and vine. From the hut a young Tamil, in a pair of greasy shorts tied up with rope, came running in long furious strides, yelling hoarsely, skidding in the dust as he seized on the fallen slippers, his voice squeezed to a long thin scream as he hurled them after her.

Still yelling, he came straight on for Simpson, who caught the incredible gleam of a knife whipped from the waist-band of the shorts.

And then the Tamil, exactly like the girl, stopped. He too seemed stunned by the relation of Simpson and the bicycle. He stood panting, spitting his surprise sideways into the dust, moving the knife in his fingers with short venomous twists at body height, at about the level of the gleaming handles of the bicycle, before he suddenly turned and walked back to the hut.

Half-way up the slope he stopped and brandished the

knife for the last time, shouting sentences Simpson had no
hope of understanding, and then disappeared.

'What was he saying?' Simpson said.

The Sikh, already turning back, one foot on the pedal of
his bicycle, shrugged his shoulders.

'Take no notice. Bad people –'

'What was it?'

'Oh! he says' – he gave the curious half-negative tilt of
the head – 'he says the knife is for Malan. But take no
notice – bad people.'

They rode back together out of the village and Simpson
was still thinking of the dipping and darting little woman,
so delicate and startled and so like Captain Custance's
description, when suddenly he saw her again.

She was lying just off the roadside, flat on her face, in the
shelter of a strip of young bamboo, waiting and watching
for him to go past. Again she was like a scared and skulking
little fowl, staring incredibly at himself and the bicycle. Her
only movement was to lift one arm to her face, framing it in
the crook of the elbow, and the last he saw of her was a sudden lowering of the arm, hiding all the face except one
bright dark eye that followed him with shocked curiosity as
he rode away.

That evening after supper – pineapples, drenched in
sticky sweetened tinned milk and sprayed with rather stale
limp nuts, had for the tenth successive night formed part of
it – Simpson sat on the veranda, thinking of Malan. A
figure built up from prejudice, from the light and shadow
of preconceptions, from the behaviour of the Chinese girl
and the voice of the shouting Tamil, from the presence
everywhere of gadgets and the toy railway, lay already complete in his mind. The man, he was quite certain, was one
of those smug inflated creatures of self-creation who are
quite unpuncturable, who inflate and re-inflate and soar in
bloated pride, endlessly, for ever. A prig: the great Malan:
the very basis of it all was in the photograph. And while
thinking he remembered the words called to him in Malay,
by the Chinese girl – O! Ka-Kăsih, Ka-Kăsih – and he

looked them up. O! Darling, O! loved one, his phrase book said.

That night, in bed, he took the photograph out again, staring at it for some minutes before he slept. And again there the fellow was: even more colossally smug, if that were possible, than when Simpson had first looked at the photograph more than a week before. Even the appalling moustache seemed, if possible, to curl a little more.

And he said, almost aloud, looking back at the girl with the pretty black hair, the fixed and fragile stare and the reputedly delicate nature:

'Well: whoever you were, I think you were well out of it. Whatever it was and whoever you are, you were well out of it. I think so.'

On Sunday Captain Custance came.

Most of the bottle of gin he brought with him was drunk, in generous portions, with lime, in the hour before lunch. Glass in hand, Captain Custance swayed about in front of the railway train, bending sometimes to feel the legs of the billiard-table underneath it as if they had been the legs of a favourite horse he had not seen for some time. 'Knock-out,' he kept saying. 'Bloody knock-out.' He winked occasionally at Simpson. At lunch, consisting of roast snipe followed by the inescapable pineapple, which Captain Custance refused, he delivered garrulous sermons with the aid of his knife and fork, banging their handles on the table.

'Wanted to tear my engine room to pieces once,' he said. 'Efficiency, more efficiency – reckoned he could replan it to give me about a hundred per cent more power. Dammit, the old tub was built in Barrow in '97 – you might as well try to make the pyramids into blocks of bloody flats. Had any trouble with the locals yet?'

'No.'

'Damn lucky. That's all. Damn lucky.'

'Shall we have coffee on the veranda?' Simpson said.

'Ought to be pushing off. Anyway I got to have one more look at that railway. That's a damnation corker. Give me a drop more gin.'

Gin in hand, Captain Custance stared again at the billiard-table and its load of flawless track and rolling stock. 'Pity,' he kept saying. 'Pity. We could have played a hundred up for a bob. Damn pity.' He became lost, in spite of himself, in admiration of Malan's remarkable handiwork, saying, loose-lipped, a little drunk: 'It's a damn marvel, y'know. Come to think of it. No flies on it. No half larks. You got to give him his due. Eh? Don't you think so?' And then:

'Seen any Chinese women yet?'

Simpson shook his head.

'Damned attractive, some of 'em. Sweet as little bantams.' Captain Custance, more garrulous than ever, seemed unaware of having said it all before. He rolled a mouthful of gin round the back of his teeth. Water moistened his reddened happy eyes. 'You ought to pick yourself one. While away the long evenings.'

'I always understood it was the thing to do.'

'Stick to you like burrs off a hedgerow,' Captain Custance said. 'Never leave you – ask the great Malan. You ask him. See what he says. Stick for ever.' It was typical of Captain Custance, in this moment of repetition, to slip on the polished floor of the billiard-room, feet skidding on a panther rug, and fall down.

By the time he was on his feet again, unsteady but unhurt, the whole question of the faithfulness of Chinese women, in reference particularly to Malan, seemed to have slipped his mind. He hobbled, belching and swearing, down to the landing-stage. Then, gin-clogged eyes shining in the sun, he shook hands several times, calling Simpson 'my boy. Remember what I said, my boy. You know?' and in a final moment of excessive affection, still looking round, fell up the gangway, from the top of which he bawled:

'I'll give you fair bloody warning when I bring him up. See what I mean? Don't want to get you caught unawares. Six toots on the Joanna – just to give you time.'

He giggled, tripped over the upper lip of the gangway and staggered in the arms of a waiting Malay.

A week later, unexpectedly, without a letter of warning from the Company and with no signal except Captain Custance's six sudden promised toots on the funnel whistle, given downstream about a mile away, Malan and his wife arrived.

The signal from Captain Custance gave Simpson just time to get down to the landing-stage. The *Roselay* was bouncing for the second time against the string of motor tyres as he passed the derelict offices where the Sikh kept chickens. A few fowls, small, brilliant-feathered, reminding him not unnaturally of Captain Custance's belief in the delicate bantam-like beauty of Chinese women but also of the fact that he had intended to clear out the chickens before Malan arrived, were scratching daintily about the dust. They rose and scattered in clouds of rosy powder as Captain Custance blew a toot of welcome on the whistle, at the same time waving his hand from his cage on the upper deck.

And then, as the *Roselay* bumped to rest, Simpson looked up. It was a moment he never forgot. Malan, stockier than he had anticipated, dressed in khaki bush-shirt and shorts, with a soft felt hat, was standing side by side with his wife, who wore a simple frock of white silk, low cut at the neck, with unelaborate crimson facings. She stood there in an attitude of such fascinated precision, too familiar to be true, that for a moment or two Simpson forgot to reply to Malan's very friendly waving hand.

Even then he could not believe, for some moments longer, that the woman on the ship was the girl in the photograph: the girl in the tennis frock, with the pretty dark hair and the engaging penetrating eyes: the girl with the delicate nature.

'Hullo there!' Malan, cordially, with easy friendliness, came down the gangway and stood on the quay and shook hands. 'Malan – no need to tell you, I'll bet, either.'

'I'm Simpson.' He was conscious of a ridiculous sensation of deference. Malan was twenty years older than himself, and he wanted suddenly, for some idiotically compelling reason, to call him sir.

'Simpson: this is my wife. We've both been looking forward no end to meeting you.'

'How do you do, Mrs Malan.'

He shook hands; she held him for a moment with the precise dark stare he knew so well from the photograph. Her hands were uncommonly small: almost out of proportion to the rest of her body, which filled the white dress to perfection, generous but compact and still young.

'Oh! not Mrs Malan: please, no Mrs,' she said. 'Eh? Not Mrs.'

'Good Heavens,' Malan said, 'no.'

'I'm Vera. What are you?'

She smiled; she looked up at him and her eyes, intense and pretty, quivered in the sun. Everything about her had the profoundly disturbing familiarity he had gleaned from the photograph.

'Bill,' he said.

'That's lovely. At least we can start right. Even if we end by hating the sight of each other.'

Malan had walked over to the edge of the landing-stage to give a final message, or perhaps simply to say good-bye to Captain Custance.

'We talked so much about you,' she said. 'Those boys at Singapore – Ford and Harrison – they talked about you all the time.' She held him with her precise dark stare. 'Very nicely too.'

A curious uneasiness, making him uncertain of himself, boyishly and self-consciously uncertain, made it impossible for him to look back at her. The *Roselay* began to move from the quay. He heard Captain Custance shout something and was glad of the chance to turn away from Mrs Malan and wave his hand.

'Well, have you been bored, waiting for us?' she said.

'No,' he said. 'That's the funny thing about it here –' he still could not look at her and, out of sheer uneasiness was watching Malan walking up from the quay – 'time seems to go terribly quickly. It's a different sort of time – it sort of dissolves away and you start forgetting –'

146

He did not know quite what he was saying; his thoughts were out of all relation to his words. He had not the slightest idea what he meant by forgetting. 'Well, as long as it always goes like that,' she said.

She started to walk up the road. He half-waited for Malan, who came up and put a hand on his shoulder: a friendly, perhaps too friendly hand, with an eager muscular squeeze.

'Well, old boy, everything all right? How does it go?'

'Very well – I'm afraid I haven't done much except learn the lingo. I'm sorry about the hens in the offices. I meant to have got them out.'

'Don't give it a thought. Plenty of pineapples?'

His sharp high laugh – like the squeeze of the hand, uncomfortable, over-eager – made Mrs Malan turn round and wait for them.

'Now what have you two got to laugh about already?'

'Oh! private joke. Eh, Bill?'

'Well –'

'Oh! now, come on. So early in the day –'

'Oh! it's nothing,' Malan said. 'You'll find out.' It was all rather forced, Simpson thought, a little brittle, not happy, besides being tedious. Mrs Malan's mouth was tight, un-relaxed in spite of its smile, in the sun, and he suddenly said:

'Look, I'll rush on and warn the Sikh about the bags and lunch. You'll want a drink too –'

He strode out up the road. Sweat prickled uneasy, like a nettle sting, all over his body, and Malan called:

'We'd specially like some pineapples. Don't forget the pineapples,' and gave once again the high overstrung laugh that was something like a crow.

At lunch Malan was like a man laying a long elaborate firing fuse. Carefully through the mulligatawny soup and its quartered limes, through the chicken and spice-hot rice, went the prepared trail that would blow, at last, the ex-plosive joke of the pineapple into Mrs Malan's face. It was like one of his gadgets, like the remarkable contraption for pulling the rattan blind: at a touch of Malan's hand the thing went up, and Malan crowed.

'Pineapples!' Mrs Malan said. The joke had not misfired. 'It's years since I really tasted one – oh! marvellous!'

'Marvellous,' Malan said. 'Jolly thoughtful of me to remember –'

'Delicious,' Mrs Malan said. 'Absolutely delicious. It couldn't be better.'

'Fresh supplies every day,' Malan said and turned to Simpson a face overjoyed, but impassive, at the success of yet another cunning device; but whether Mrs Malan too was aware of it, or not aware of it, or simply too used to it to care, he did not know.

'What about this labour situation?' Malan said. Lunch was over and the three of them were sitting, with coffee, on the veranda. Sometimes across the clearing, once a garden but now a pink arena of dust where fowls scratched, large butterflies of narcissus cream and yellow danced with great trembling strokes to disappear into the bamboo fringe beyond. Entranced, Mrs Malan gave an occasional cry of gasping, sighing delight at such loveliness; and at last, unable to bear the sight of a floating triangle of more lovely, more unreal brilliance than the rest, she got up and walked after it, stalking it, stealthily, like a child in the sun.

Malan was glad of the opportunity to slip over and sit in the chair next to Simpson.

'We must get this labour organized. What were you able to do? Any luck at all?'

'No,' Simpson said. 'No work. That's what they say.'

'I see,' Malan said, 'I'd better go down there. Soon as possible. This afternoon.'

Out in the compound Mrs Malan had kicked off her shoes and was running with naked feet after butterflies.

'Put your shoes on!' Malan called. 'You want to get foot worm or some other damn thing?'

Out in the dust, small, intense-eyed, and hurt, she was caught in pained surprise by the sharp crow of Malan's voice.

'Put them on!'

'Are you speaking to me?' she said.

'Put your shoes on and do as you're told and don't argue.
Never run about without your shoes in this country.'

'All the natives do –'

'You're not a native. Put them on.'

An air of intense pain, of deeply injured affection not
defiant but transfixed so that it gave her eyes exactly the
appearance, very close together, of the double holes of a
gun-barrel, held her there absolutely motionless for perhaps
another fifteen or twenty seconds. Her shoes lay in the dust
and Simpson, watching them, remembered the slippers of
the little Chinese woman and how, like little scarlet tongues,
they had lain in the dust too.

'You know what you promised.'

'Yes,' she said.

She put on her shoes.

Malan, taking a sip of coffee and leaning over again to
Simpson, said nothing beyond a casual, almost curt remark
in explanation:

'She's rather delicate. She has to take care,' and then:

'Yes, I think I'd better go down there. By the way I've
got letters for you –'

'I'll come down too,' Simpson said.

'No. I'll go alone. It's better. It's probably going to be
frightfully tricky and it would be simpler if I nipped down
myself on the bike.'

'By the way, I've been using your bicycle. The Sikh
said –'

'Oh! you have, have you?'

That afternoon Malan was gone for three hours. Simpson
spent most of the afternoon rearranging his things. He had
slept for three weeks in the large bedroom, now to be
occupied by Mr and Mrs Malan, but without fans to work
and cool the air he had found it very hot indoors and now
he decided to sleep on the veranda, in a small camp bed.

'Are you really going to sleep there? Aren't you worried
about things creeping about?'

All afternoon Mrs Malan kept up a flow of pleasant, idly personal conversation.

'I should be worried stiff, sleeping out there. Is it always as hot as this?'

'Always. You ought to rest in the afternoons,' he said. 'You'll find it pays.'

'Oh! I'm too excited to rest. The first day and all that, you know – how long are you going to be here?'

'I don't quite know. Perhaps another month,' he said. 'The idea was to send me to a plantation farther north –'

'Spencer said if you were any good he'd like to keep you here. That's if you wanted to –'

Spencer – it took him some seconds to grasp that she was using Malan's Christian name. Spencer Malan: it was like the name of an actor, a priest, an explorer or something. It had importance. It was incredible and yet it fitted him rather well.

Mrs Malan too had been unpacking her things. At four o'clock the Sikh brought tea on to the veranda and Simpson, tapping on the open door of her bedroom and entering in answer to her voice, found her surrounded by the gay curtaining of many dresses on coat-hangers, night-gowns lying on the bed, silk stockings and feathery, flimsy lingerie spilling over chair. That array of soft pretty clothing seemed to heighten all her delicacy. At the door, seeing them, he hesitated a moment but she said, 'Oh! come in, come in. Don't mind all this,' turning on him a pair of direct dark eyes with the curious magnetic precision he had seen so often in the photograph.

That personal intimate glimpse of all her clothing lying about them gave him his first touch of heightened feeling about her. She was holding in her hands, as he came in, a chiffon night-gown, a soft yellow, rather the colour of the butterfly she had chased across the compound, and looking as if made, almost, of the same flimsy transparent stuff.

He could not help looking at it. She saw him looking and smiled and held it across her body. 'Isn't it nice?' she said.

'Isn't it lovely?' and smoothed it down, across the front of her breasts, with one hand, smiling again.

His heart started racing wildly and she said:

'I've got the loveliest things. I determined I would have. I determined I wouldn't come out here and be sloppy and look like a frump just because there weren't other women here.' She laid the nightdress on the bed and the revelation of her clothed body underneath it – she had somehow given the impression that it was all she had on – gave him a curious shock. 'What about you?' she said. 'Have you got a girl?'

'No.' he said. 'By the way there's tea on the veranda now –'

'I bet you have,' she said. 'Somewhere.'

'No,' he said. 'No.'

'You've got a photograph of her too. Show me the photograph.'

'No, really,' he said. A small quivering hammer made staccato stabbings just under his heart. 'No honestly – it's true –'

'You'll show me it later,' she said. 'Men always do.'

Out on the veranda, pouring tea, slipping into each cup a quarter of lime like a little brilliant emerald-yellow boat, carefully and delicately, she said:

'Some tea? How many sugars? It's awfully hot, isn't it? You've gone quite pale.'

That evening, at supper, Malan talked mostly about the electricity. In a couple of days he would have it working. The Sikh had been very good, keeping the generator clean and dry – the Sikhs were fond of engineering and that sort of thing, good mechanics – and Malan would give it the final overhaul to-morrow. He hoped to fit a silencer to it, so that the noise would not be too bad. In any case it did not need to run for many hours at a time. The demands on it were very limited: just the lighting, the fans, the refrigerator and –

'Of course the train,' he said.

Simpson thought Mrs Malan, staring cross-wise, in a

dreamy oblique sort of way, between himself and Malan, did not seem in any way interested in the train.

'We'll open the track next Sunday,' Malan said. 'Break a bottle on it or something. And mind, no peeping till then –'

'I wouldn't dream of peeping,' she said, her voice innocent and thin and cool.

'Make it a party when Captain Custance comes,' Simpson said. The words came to him without thinking. There was the strangest sort of tension in the air between Malan and his wife that he could not explain. 'Custance,' he said with sudden eagerness, 'is dying to see it working –'

'You showed it to Custance?' Malan said – he looked affronted rather than annoyed – 'that nosey old rascal –'

Simpson, embarrassed, could think of nothing to say. Mrs Malan looked tense. Malan broke into a harsh splintering crackle the remains of a water-biscuit and the situation was saved a moment later by the entry of the Sikh, proudly bringing the inevitable dishes of pineapple and whipped milk and pistachio as if they were offerings either to or from the gods, and Mrs Malan finished the tension with a final cry:

'Pineapple! That's just what I want to quench my thirst.'

Malan, in that moment, did a curious thing, followed a second later by another. He winked swiftly at Simpson, all trace of resentment or affront or annoyance gone, and then got up from the table, replacing his chair.

'What's the matter? Don't you want your pineapple? Where are you going?'

'I'm worried about this labour thing,' Malan said. 'I'm going over to see Bruno.'

'Bruno? Who's Bruno?'

'He used to be one of my boys. He's got a lot of influence in the village – his brother-in-law's a trader. I tried to get him this afternoon but he was fishing up-river. He'll probably have a few fish I can bring back –'

'Don't be long.'

As he came past her she held his hand, lifting her face, and he stooped to kiss her.

'Have coffee with Bill on the veranda. It's cooler out there. Bill will look after you.'

'Don't stay long,' she said and gave him, as he went out of the door, a wonderfully intent and pressing smile that reacted on Simpson with a start of pain.

Later, as they sat on the veranda, in darkness broken only by the reflection through the windows of the lamp burning in the dining-room, she sat in a cane chair some distance away from him, the table between them, and for some time there was hardly a sound from her but the creak of the chair and the occasional clink of her cup and coffee spoon. He was glad, for a time, that she had nothing to say. The night was full of a heavy plush-like beauty, with uncommonly brilliant and enormous stars. Everywhere there was a depth of darkness and scintillation, of purple and blackness, with flashes of fire and emerald, and a silence of impenetrable wonder that was almost grandeur as it folded profoundly away. He had sat alone, almost every night, like this, listening to the silence, feeling it about him like an enormous pulse-beat, and now it was more beautiful because there was someone to share it with him who had the sense not to break it with foolish words. He turned his head slightly and looked at her in the chair. He could see her hands, fine and delicate and small, on the edges of the chair, and her arms golden-white, not yet burned by sun, naked to the shoulder. Her breasts were mature and full, thrown out a little by the attitude of her body in the chair, her head leaning backwards, the outer edges of her black hair ignited to a flush of brightness from the glow of the lamp behind her.

At last she turned her head very slightly towards him and said:

'I thought you'd gone to sleep, you're so quiet. There was something I wanted to ask you.'

'Yes,' he said.

'Perhaps it sounds silly –'

He waited, staring at the stars.

'Is there something funny about pineapples?' she said. 'Is it a joke with you?'

'No.'

'It's a joke, isn't it?'

'Not exactly.'

'Why is it a joke? Is it from something I said?'

He was surprised by a start of inner rage against Malan. It was so violent that it constricted his voice as he began to try to explain away the monstrously stupid business of the pineapples.

It was only that there were so many, he explained. They were a plague, just an indestructible weed. You couldn't get rid of them. The Sikh served them twice or three times a day and at first you thought they were wonderful but after a time they were like poison and you wanted to scream. That was all it was.

She listened in silence. He felt a glow of immense pity for her rise out of his now subdued anger against Malan. She moved at last, speaking in a distant way, quietly.

'Thank you,' she said. And then: 'There was something else I wanted to ask you.'

'Yes,' he said.

'Will you tell me if you see I am making a fool of myself again? Will you tell me that?'

'I'm sure there won't be any need.'

'I don't want to make a fool of myself,' she said. 'Will you tell me?'

'Yes,' he said.

'You're very sweet,' she said. 'Remember – I rely on you.'

After that she did not speak again until, perhaps twenty minutes later, she said, 'I'm getting sleepy. I think I must go in,' and got up from her chair. He got up too but she said, 'Don't get up. Please,' but it was too late and he found himself standing a few inches away from her, his gaze held for a second or two by the glowing magnetic stare of the small black eyes and then, suddenly lowering, of the crossward fold of her dress over her breasts. 'Good night,' she said.

The palms of his hands were sweating as he shook hands. He had not expected to shake hands. Her formal cool uplifted hand brought her an inch or so closer and then she drew it away. It was as fresh and smooth in texture as the skin of a fruit. 'Sleep well,' she said.

He walked as far as the jetty, standing there for some time listening to the river advancing sea-ward in wide breaking flood-swirls that struck at banks and tree-roots in a fish-bone series of little waves. He smoked a final cigarette and looked at the stars and thought of Mrs Malan. He could not tell what lay behind that appeal about making a fool of herself and that rather desperate remark of hers: 'Remember – I rely on you.' All the inside of himself melted in a strange fluidity of engrossed and tender wonder as he thought of her and tried, youthful and fascinated, to work it out.

When he got back to his bungalow the Sikh was still up, waiting to lock the doors. 'Malan not in?' Simpson said and George, in a sharp, almost defiant flick, shook his head.

Afterwards he lay awake for a long time on his small camp-bed, under the mosquito net, thinking. In the Malans' bedroom the lamp continued to burn, keeping him awake even when he turned at last and tried to sleep, and Malan did not come in.

In two days, as Malan had promised, the electricity began to work. Lights, fans, refrigerator: there was an infinity of useful switches everywhere. By day, for two or three hours, the generator added to the discomfort of stunning midday heat a coughing brain-beating thud.

To the multitude of household gadgets Malan added an astounding, admirable efficiency in bigger things. Soon the offices were cleared of chickens; and an overhead cable, insulated on high poles of bamboo, took power for fans and light down from the bungalow, and the estate plan found its place over Malan's big teak desk on the wall. 'I've got the idea for inter-comm. speakers all worked out too,' Malan said, 'so that if we want each other or a boy or anything we don't have to go running and yelling round. You've got to save the sweat here.'

Simpson found himself full of reluctant admiration; the curious moment of hatred did not obtrude again. Once, from the far side of the estate, down to the landing-stage, a narrow gauge railway had run. Time, with the coming of motor transport, seemed to have made it obsolete, but Malan did not agree. 'Easier and cheaper to run. Quieter and never dusty. Trucks going past the bungalow would be hell for us. No, we'll get it going again. All we need is the labour.'

'You're rather fond of little trains, aren't you?' Simpson said.

'Oh! that? You mean the other one? I built that when I was here alone. You have to have something to amuse yourself when you're alone.'

The question of labour was something that Simpson finally thought it tactful to leave alone. Two or three Tamils appeared and assisted the laying of cables from the bungalow to the offices, but when he inquired of Malan how soon the coolies would be coming in anything like useful numbers Malan gave one of the sudden curt replies that had crushed the inquisitiveness of Captain Custance:

'I'll deal with the labour. That's my pigeon. Never worry your head in this climate about things that are supposed to worry other people. That's the quickest way to belly-trouble.'

'I just thought –'

'Well, don't think. Thinking is bad in this climate.'

'I know the thing is a headache,' Simpson said. 'The way you're out there nearly every night trying to get it straightened out –'

'I'll straighten it,' Malan said. 'I've straightened it before. Do your work. Never mind where I go at night or for that matter at any other time. That's my affair.'

One morning, after breakfast, Simpson felt a thickness about his eyes; the whites of them were yellow and liverish and there was a dull beating, made worse by the Sikh's breakfast of fried eggs, on the bone of the forehead. He stayed behind for a time after breakfast, bathing his head with lumps of ice in the bath-house, and when he reached the offices Malan was already working.

'Late,' Malan said.

'I felt a bit seedy.'

Malan caught him by the jaw in a movement that ejected his tongue a second before he had said the word.

'I told you you'd get belly-trouble,' he said. 'This your first touch of gyppy tummy?'

'Yes.'

'Go back and tell Vera to give you chlorodyne and one of the tablets in the yellow bottles – she'll know. You'll be all right after a bit – it's nothing, you'll be all right.'

Back at the bungalow Mrs Malan was sitting on the veranda, writing letters.

'I thought you looked off-colour at breakfast,' she said, and he was pleased, comforted in his grey liverish state, to think that she had noticed it.

She mixed the chlorodyne for him in a tumbler and stood watching him with intent dark eyes as he drank the sweetish soothing milk of it.

'You ought to take a day off,' she said. 'You look all in.'

He shook his head; something bumped under his skull like a leaden ball.

'How's your pulse?' she said. 'Come here – let me feel it.' In expert fingers she quietly held his hand. 'I used to be a nurse. During the war. I was nursing Spencer when –'
She broke off, looking at the watch on her wrist.

It was her first noticeable sign of uneasiness about Malan. It struck him strangely: the quick, mistaken glance at the watch, born of habit and now prompted by nervousness, as if she were taking his temperature as well as his pulse.

He had an idea suddenly, also, that she was not even counting his pulse. The fingers were there, resting on his throbbing blood; but the mind was not there. For some reason he knew she was distracted, far away.

'It's all right,' she said. 'I'll take your temperature at lunch. The thermometer's packed away somewhere.'

'It's nothing – I'll work it off,' he said.

As he reached the end of the veranda she called to him:
'By the way, have you a key to the billard-room?'

'Yes.' It was part of Malan's general habit of efficiency
that each of them should have, except for purely personal
things, a key for everything.

'Would you lend it me?'

'Yes: of course,' he said.

She smiled and said, 'Thank you. I'll give it back to-
night.'

In the evening he felt better. After supper Malan stayed
for a short time on the veranda to take coffee and then,
as on so many other nights, excused himself and walked
down the road. She lay quiet in her chair; she might have
been listening to his footsteps retreating down the pink-dust
road between the wilderness of rampant pineapples. She
seemed to judge the quietness carefully for five minutes
longer and then her arm came out from the chair.

'The key,' she said.

'Thank you.' He took his wallet from the breast pocket of
his bush-shirt. An aunt, efficient too in her kindly way, had
given him a farewell present of a new wallet with a neat
compartment for keys: better than wearing out the linings
of his trousers pocket, she said.

He opened the wallet to put in the key and suddenly,
before he could prevent it, she swung both hands across and
clutched it.

'Let me see,' she said. 'The photo of your girl's in it. I
know it is – let me see.'

'Oh! no, please –'

'Come on,' she said. 'Own up – let me see.'

She twisted her body, sitting on the edge of his chair, half-
wrenching the wallet from him. The chair rocked danger-
ously, tipping over at an angle with the weight of two bodies.
He put out a hand to check it, touching the wooden floor-
slats, and in that moment she slipped and fell against him.
He felt the smooth shape of her leg fleshily touching his own,
the weight of her breast, unsteadied by her hands, falling
across his arm. He let go the wallet, tipping the chair back

into balance so that with the motion of it she was rocked back, laughing, against him.

It was a laugh of triumph that teased him too: because now she had the wallet and he did not stop her. He could feel the shape of her body outlined against his knee. There was a little light from the lamp in the dining-room and she turned her back to him, opening the wallet, so that she could look at it. Her hair, fired at the back by light, was scalloped into long and brilliant edges of dense black curls, and he was fired too by the frenzy of watching it, so close that he could touch it with his mouth. He knew that in a moment he would touch it with his mouth and then draw her back, by the throat; he knew that she could only have come to him like that because she wanted to come, soft and deliberate and laughing and excited, and because she wanted to be near him and because she wanted him to draw her down; and then he heard her gasp, softly:

'Good God: how did you come by this? Where *did* you get it?'

A day or two before he had cut the picture in half, throwing Malan away.

'I found it here.'

'But it's ancient – years old – ghastly –'

He held her gently by the throat, drawing her back until her face was level with his own. His wallet fell away somewhere, slipping down the unencumbered silky front of her body and clattering with its keys on the veranda floor. She did not say a word. A twist of her body brought her half round to him, so that she lay across him, turning her face. Her mouth in another moment was full against his and fire, in a series of running, beating waves, ran wildly up through him as she kissed him, almost hurting him with the fixed long strength of it.

'Fancy me,' she said, 'me – how was it me?'

'Who else?' he said.

'Oh! God,' she said and he saw, as in the photograph just so minutely and with just such precision, but now so in-flamed and so profoundly dark that he could hardly bear to

look at them, the deep eyes staring and holding him transfixed.

In another moment, in a loud whisper, quite loud enough,
he thought, for Malan to hear if he were coming up the
road, she called him darling, and instinctively he turned to
look in the direction Malan would come.

'Let's walk to the river,' he said, 'it's better there. In
case –'

'No,' she said; she spoke in the quietest compelling sort of
breath, almost a sigh, her lips just brushing his face. 'No,
here. Here will do. It's better here –'

He kissed her again, searching the front of her body excitedly with his hands, feeling its full tautness, the lovely
nest-like hollow, without a word of protest from her.

'You're not afraid of anything, are you?' she said.
'You're not afraid?'

'No, not afraid,' he said. He felt her trembling with excitement and joy. 'Not afraid.'

After that, every evening she would wait for him on the
veranda, swinging quietly in her chair until Malan had
gone. Every evening, she wore a different dress. The two
meals of the day at which the three of them were together,
the evening one especially, became more and more of a pain,
and sometimes he could not bear to look at her. Yet whenever he did look she was always looking in return: with that
delicate undisturbed precision of hers, quiet and magnetic
and powerful, holding him completely. It never failed.

The curious thing was that he could not help feeling it
was directed just as much at Malan. At first that part of it
troubled him. Then he got over it; he saw that of course,
naturally, there had to be a smile for Malan too. Deception
as well as love had to have its smile. He even grew used to
her lifting her face to Malan, to take his kisses; he could even
ignore, almost, the fondness of the departing word:

'Don't be long, dear. Please.'

On the question of the labour force Simpson now waited
a cue from Malan. It appeared one evening that Malan was

worried by communists: 'That's half the trouble here. They're infiltrating everywhere. They're the trouble makers. They don't want you to have labour – prevent it by every damn means in their power.'

'You think there'll be trouble?' Simpson said. 'I mean –'

'Not bandits?' she said.

'Good God no. It's a local thing. They're like children – they need soothing gently.'

'Anyway Bill's an awfully good shot, aren't you, Bill? Bill can take care of me.'

'I know. I want him to.'

'In fact I think he takes care of me better than you do.'

'Good,' Malan said. 'That's what I like to hear.'

Serenely, with a sort of stiff innocence that chilled him with terror, she put her arm into Simpson's as they walked from the dining-room. 'He's a very good escort.' Her eyes held Malan with the most engaging frigid charm. 'He's very good to me. Aren't you jealous? He spoils me.'

'I'm not jealous.'

'Then you ought to be.' She quite snapped the words, hard and short, and her face coloured up. 'Men don't deserve to have nice wives if they're not jealous of them.'

Malan grinned; nothing of that curious conversation, which chilled and horrified Simpson so much that he felt his breath locked in his throat, seemed to affect him.

'I'm not jealous,' was all he said. 'I wouldn't know how to be.'

'Come on, Bill,' she said. 'There's no arguing with some people.'

That evening, on the veranda still flooded with light from the electric lamps in the dining-room, she kissed him even before Malan had gone. It was as if she could not wait to be held by him. She called him darling several times in a voice loud enough for Malan to hear. All the time he could hear Malan himself talking to the Sikh on some question of fixing the silencer to the generator, and a few words of Malan came distinctly to him on the quiet air.

'For God's sake,' he whispered.

'Oh! darling,' she said loudly. 'Who cares?'

'Please,' he said.

'I want you so terribly to-night.' Her voice was contained in a high frenzied sort of whisper that seemed to carry better than a shout. 'I can't bear it –'

A moment later Malan came on to the veranda, carrying his rifle. There was hardly a word that could not have been heard, Simpson thought, and Mrs Malan was still standing so close to him that it would not have been surprising if Malan had shot them. Instead he said, swiftly:

'Well, I'll be off. The coffee will be along in a moment. I kept the Sikh talking –'

'Why the rifle?' she said.

'I just thought it might be policy to show that we could shoot if necessary, that's all.'

'Isn't it a bit provocative?' Simpson said. In a confusion of nerves he felt a new insecure sort of hatred for the too-sure, too-efficient Malan.

'Not more than most things,' Malan said, and walked away.

He had hardly walked a hundred yards down the road before she came to sit with him in the chair. She kissed him once but she seemed uneasy and suddenly she said:

'It's awfully hot to-night. I'll go and put on my house-coat – it's hotter than ever –'

He heard her go through the house, calling the Sikh to delay the coffee until she rang the bell. He was nervous and actually got up and walked a few yards beyond the end of the veranda, standing there to listen, half-expecting Malan to come back. But there was nothing: only the customary pulsing silence, hot with suspense beating at the darkness.

When she came back she had put on a house-coat of flowered crimson and yellow silk. She rang the bell – another of Malan's efficient little gadgets for saving steps and sweat – and then half-lay, half-sat with Simpson in the cane long-chair, waiting for the coffee to come. And when the

Sikh came at last on soft feet to bring the tray she did not get up. She lay there all the time, her face close to Simpson's, while the Sikh poured the coffee.

'You ought to be a little careful,' he said. The Sikh had gone and in the dining-room all but one of the lights had been put out. It poured its bright shaft on her eager, excited face.

'Why?' she said. 'I'm excited – I can't wait for you. Don't you want me too?'

'Terribly,' he said, and let himself be drawn down, feeling the unencumbered tautness of her body pressing up against him through the silk of the house-coat as the loose flaps of the coat fell away.

Every night he was persuaded that the stars grew more exceptional in brilliance and beauty than the night before. That night they seemed to stab down in great pulses of emerald and ruby and orange, in surges of bright loveliness that matched the burst of his own feelings as he lay with her first in the chair and then, for another hour, on his bed. In the moment when her house-coat fell away and he felt the first touch of her body naked and free he remembered the day he had seen her unpacking her things. Her nightdress had fallen away from her body that day in much the same way and he had been shot through by the sharp beauty of it, the bright consciousness of seeing her really for the first time. He had wondered what her body was like; and in a way it had been inevitable to wonder and at last to find out, and now it was his.

Later that evening, quieter, in a deadly, rather far-off voice, she spoke with great bitterness of Malan:

'If it hadn't been for me he wouldn't have been here. I nursed him for six months. He was in one of those bomb-disposal units – no heroics, you know, just more gadgets – and something went off too soon. Eight of them were killed and he was a wreck. If it hadn't been for me fighting for him – fighting all the time –'

'I'll get transferred to another company,' he said. 'We'll get out of this.'

She seemed to take no notice of that; she seemed wrapped in hatred of Malan.

'The way you can fight for people – go on fighting too –'

He felt her hatred become his own. All that he had gathered in that quaint period of pre-conception about Malan had, after all, turned out to be true: the gadget king, the oracle, the man who had been and seen and conquered before, the prig of experience, the great Malan. Hatred, not bitter but more allied in its hot surges with his feeling for her, rushed through him, taking the last of his reticence and caution with it.

'If only we could get away,' he said. 'Somehow we have to get away – we simply have to get away –'

'It's a queer thing, love,' she said, as if once again she were not really noticing what he said, 'the way it drives you and beats you,' and above him, he thought, the stars seemed to explode in fragmentary and more lovely, more brilliant cascades than ever before. He had never seen such stars.

The Sikh woke him at five o'clock, half an hour earlier than usual, muttering hoarsely.

'Trouble,' he said. 'There is much trouble. Malan Sahib –'

Out in the compound one of the Tamil boys stood crouched and trembling in the rose-grey sunless daylight.

Together Simpson, the Sikh and the Tamil boy cycled down to the village. There was not much to be done. Malan was lying on the earth floor of a palm-hut with a knife slit deep down the side of the neck and cutting into the shoulder.

Simpson stood outside the hut, sick, trying to collect himself, staring at the sun coming up beyond the deserted roofs of palm and corrugated iron. He started to say something about communists, about the bandits beginning at last.

'No, no, no,' the Sikh said. 'No, no –'

Simpson, remembering the little Chinese woman running to greet him on the path below, had nothing to say. He was still trembling so much on the way back that he could not ride the bicycle. He pushed it slowly along, his mouth so parched that he was even glad to stop, by the ramping grey-blue cactus wilderness, and ask the Sikh to cut him a pine-apple. He buried his face in it as eagerly as he had done on the very first day.

At the bungalow he walked up and down outside for some time, smoking a cigarette to calm himself before he went in. He was aware of a queer distorted sort of triumph waiting for him in the moment when he came to tell her. Not the great Malan now: only the dead Malan. Queer that for a second time – and not only queer but a miracle – something had misfired.

When he went into the bedroom to speak to her she was still asleep. He sat on the edge of the bed, looking at her as she began to wake up. She was wearing the white night-dress and sleep had crumpled it. He could see her breasts clear and pink through the bodice of it and suddenly he wanted to sit there on the edge of the bed, not telling her but only touching her with his hands. He wanted terribly to take her in the first free moment that they had had together. It would be time to tell her afterwards.

'Darling,' she said, 'what are you doing here? What time is it? Don't you feel well again? You've gone quite pale.'

He began to tell her as simply as he could. He had deter-mined to make up a line about it. It was very simple: the communists, the bandits, had begun at last. She lay watch-ing him with big fixed incredulous eyes and it was only when he spoke of communists that she seemed really to wake up, to understand what he was trying to say.

She sat up and yelled at him:

'Don't tell me lies! Don't try and tell me lies! What happened? Who killed him? – I don't want lies.'

'Communists –'

'It was the woman, wasn't it?' she shouted. 'The Tamil – I know, I know. I knew all the time.'

'Look,' he said. 'We're not certain. It's no use probing into detail. I know how you feel –'

She jumped out of bed and screamed at him starkly:

'Don't stand there talking like a raving fool! How do you know how I feel? How can you know?'

Shocked, not knowing what to say, he stretched out his hands and tried to hold her. She beat them away, shouting for him not to touch her. Her eyes were tearless and brilliant and hateful and suddenly he had an awful feeling. It was that all the bitterness she had felt about Malan was being turned, more violently now, on him.

'I'm terribly sorry,' he said. 'Don't upset yourself. It's awful, I know – but it sets us free –'

'Free?' she yelled at him. 'Who wants to be free?'

He stood coldly, stunned, in the centre of the room. She was trying to drag on her house-coat. In her haste the zip had locked, so that she could not get it working. He stood helplessly looking on as she struggled and then suddenly she looked up and saw his lost, stupefied face and shouted:

'What do you think I came out here for? I knew all about it. I wanted him back! – I wanted him! – He never wanted me to come! –'

Her patience with the zip ended suddenly and the coat did not matter any longer. She pitched forward on the bed and lay there beating the pillow with her hands.

'Oh! God, darling, why didn't you listen to me? Why didn't you listen? For God's sake why didn't you listen to me?'

While she still lay there he walked out of the room and sat on the veranda. The sun was coming up brilliant and fiercely white. Once again the leaden ball had begun to swing heavily under his skull and he sat for a long time with his head in his hands.

After a time she came out of her room and yelled for the key of the billiard-room. He gave it her without speaking. She rushed away and he heard her, in hysteria, smashing up the model railway.

That was his only moment of gladness, and he did not stop her.

Two days later they went down-river, with Captain

Custance, in the *Roselay*. She had taken on a rigid distant calmness and spent most of her time in the cabin, lying down.

At noon a Malay seaman rang the bell for lunch and Simpson went down to the stifling stove-hot little saloon. She was not there and after waiting a moment or two he went down the narrow passage to where she was lying in the cabin. He tapped on the door and called her name.

'Come in,' she said.

He went in and stood looking at her, saying quietly: 'Lunch is ready. Do you want lunch?' knowing that she would say no.

'Something to drink?' he said.

'No.'

'It's cooler up above. You'll find it cooler than here.'

'I'm all right here.'

Two impulses flowed quickly through him. He wanted to touch her, with all possible tenderness, as she lay there in the narrow wooden bunk under the open port-hole. He wanted to revive, as gently as possible, the feeling he thought she had shown for him that evening on the veranda, before Malan had died.

'Do you remember asking me about making a fool of yourself?' he said.

'That was only because I knew he didn't want me.'

'Do you mind if I ask you something now?' he said.

'What?' she said.

'Do you love me?'

'No,' she said.

'Do you want me?'

'I think you're very sweet,' she said. 'It couldn't have happened if you hadn't been so sweet.'

She held him for a moment or two longer with the minutely precise stare that had first captivated him in the photograph. The little cabin shuddered heavily, under the strain of engine revolutions, and it was as if, for a moment, her face quivered. But he knew that it did not quiver. It did not respond to him any more than the brown-yellow river he could see flowing past the port-hole above her head.

'I wanted to know before we landed,' he said. 'I wanted to put a bit of a face on it, you see.'

He waited for a moment longer to see if she would answer. She did not answer. It occurred to him that she would, perhaps, say that she was sorry; but she did not say it. She lay with dark eyes minutely staring, and presently he went on deck, telling the steward that he did not want to eat as he went through the saloon.

He stood for some time with Captain Custance on the bridge. The *Roselay* had moved faster down-river than he had expected and now, through the carmine and emerald elbows of forest, he caught his first glimpse of open sea. The river was running fast, fanning out ahead with the strong silt-brown tide, discolouring the flat cobalt-vivid ocean.

'Hellish tricky here sometimes,' Captain Custance said. 'I knew a master once who laid a ship up through taking her too close here. Looks wider than it is. It was blowing smoke at the time.'

In an ensuing moment or two of silence he gathered spittle, chewing on it as if it were hard india-rubber.

'Taking it as well as could be expected?'

'Yes.'

'Bloody rum go. Bloody rum. You could have knocked me down with a pint-pot when I saw her coming aboard.' He rattled on, chewing his words, relaxing to gather spittle that was never ejected, his words glib in sailor-wise fashion, gossipy, not meaning much, his eyes on the open sea.

'Well, he bought it. That's all I can say. He bought it. He's been buying it for a long time. Everybody up the river knew he'd been buying it for a long time.'

Simpson stared ahead too at the open sea: sterile, not thinking, swiftly watching the river dirt discolour in its brown fan the vivid outer cobalt of sunlit water. The heat on the nape of his neck had all the stunning, bruising force of mid-afternoon.

'Lucky you happened to be there,' Captain Custance

said. 'Bit of luck or God knows what she would have done without you.'

Simpson, intent on the fusion of river and open sea, was not listening. The *Roselay*, caught in powerful twists of estuary currents, shuddered once again, as Captain Custance had said before, like a bloody factory. But there was a sudden breath of relief, a stir of sea-wind, clean and salty in spite of heat, that bore away in a refreshing moment the stupefying steamy heat of the river.

He looked down, a moment later, to see Mrs Malan on deck, standing in the bows. His impulses of tenderness started up again, waving away his sterility. He felt he wanted to go down and ask her, for the last time, if she had anything left for him, a trace of something, the smallest thing. He saw the wind from the open sea blow her dress against her legs and a stir of it, with sun, inflame into scalloped gold-black edges the fringe of her hair.

He knew it was only Malan she wanted: the dead Malan, back there, the efficient Spencer, the gadget king, the oracle who had been and done it all before, the prig: the great Malan. She had exterminated everything for that, extinguished it all: distance, time, all the others, the rivals and himself. It was all as obvious as it would ever need to be.

After a few moments he could bear it no longer. He went down to the deck and stood by the rail of the ship, close to her.

'May I talk again?' he said. 'Do you mind if I talk?'

'No.'

A queer involuntary moment of agony locked his throat, choking him. The *Roselay* seemed to sweep a long way to open sea before he could speak again:

'I can't bear it without you.'

She did not answer.

He put one hand across her shoulders, smoothing her bare arm. It was rigid and smoothly neutral, but she did not draw it away. At the touch of her body fires of tenderness began leaping up in him again, reaching his eyes in small tears, so that he was dazzled by the running rose-brown tide of open sea.

'Don't make me let you go,' he said. 'I can't bear it – I can't let you go.'

He touched her throat very softly and she turned her head for the first time, looking at him with the old minute precision, clear and inexorable and dissecting.

'I didn't expect you would let me go.'

Joy shot through him and it was as if also, at the same moment, the *Roselay* shot forward, almost out of the river currents, clear at last.

'Oh! I love you,' he began to say.

He could feel the softest regular pulsing of the blood in her throat. 'I'd do anything –'

'You know now,' she said. 'You know now how it feels.'

He did not answer. He could feel her body soft and pulsing and yet distant under his hand. He watched the sea, running now from brown to green and beyond, all pure in scintillation, a beautiful light cobalt that was like the sky. He wanted to think that he was clear and free himself and that now, at last, she belonged to him.

And yet it was not what he was thinking. He could think only of the eyes in the photograph: the small dark eyes, with their timeless, penetrating precision, the beautiful, relentless eyes – and behind them, always, the delicate nature.

MORE ABOUT PENGUINS, PELICANS
AND PUFFINS

For further information about books available from Penguins please write to Dept EP, Penguin Books Ltd, Harmondsworth, Middlesex UB7 ODA.

In the U.S.A.: For a complete list of books available from Penguins in the United States write to Dept DG, Penguin Books, 299 Murray Hill Parkway, East Rutherford, New Jersey 07073.

In Canada: For a complete list of books available from Penguins in Canada write to Penguin Books Canada Ltd, 2801 John Street, Markham, Ontario L3R 1B4.

In Australia: For a complete list of books available from Penguins in Australia write to the Marketing Department, Penguin Books Australia Ltd, P.O. Box 257, Ringwood, Victoria 3134.

In New Zealand: For a complete list of books available from Penguins in New Zealand write to the Marketing Department, Penguin Books (N.Z.) Ltd, P.O. Box 4019, Auckland 10.

In India: For a complete list of books available from Penguins in India write to Penguin Overseas Ltd, 706 Eros Apartments, 56 Nehru Place, New Delhi 110019.

H. E. Bates was one of the most popular and best-loved novelists of recent years. The following are some of the novels and stories published in Penguins.

THE TRIPLE ECHO

H. E. Bates tells movingly the strange tale of a lonely woman and her love affair with a young deserter, of their intrigues and their deceptions and the elaborate web they weave to outwit the Military Police.

THE FOUR BEAUTIES

Four novellas, *The Simple Life; The Four Beauties; The Chords of Youth* and *The White Wind*, that reveal Bates's knowledge of human relationships.

SEVEN BY FIVE

Subtle, passionate, tantalizing and direct, H. E. Bates explores the English character and scene from the mid-twenties to the early sixties. This collection of stories bears witness to his claim to be master of the English short story.

FAIR STOOD THE WIND FOR FRANCE

'Perhaps the finest novel of the war ... The scenes are exquisitely done and the characters – tenderly and beautifully drawn – are an epitome of all that is best in the youth of the two countries. This is a fine, lovely book which makes the heart beat with pride' – *Daily Telegraph*

THE WILD CHERRY TREE

In each of these ten stories H. E. Bates evokes places and defines a life full of oddities and curiosities you could never before have imagined.

H. E. Bates's Best-Selling 'Larkin' Books

THE DARLING BUDS OF MAY

Introducing the Larkins, a family with a place in popular mythology.

Here they come, in the first of their hilarious rural adventures, crashing their way through the English countryside in the wake of Pa, the quick-eyed golden-hearted junk-dealer, and Ma, with a mouthful of crisps and a laugh like a jelly.

A BREATH OF FRENCH AIR

They're here again – the indestructible Larkins; this time, with Baby Oscar, the Rolls, and Ma's unmarried passport, they're off to France. And with H. E. Bates, you may be sure, there's no French without tears of laughter.

WHEN THE GREEN WOODS LAUGH

In the third of the Larkin novels H. E. Bates makes the Dragon's Blood and the double scotches hit with no less impact than they did in *The Darling Buds of May*. For the full Larkin orchestra is back on the rural fiddle, and (with Angela Snow around) the Brigadier may be too old to ride but he's young enough to fall.

OH! TO BE IN ENGLAND

Are you taking life too seriously?

What you need is a dose of *Oh! To Be in England* – another splendid thighs-breasts-and-buttercups frolic through the Merrie England of the sixties with the thirsty, happy, lusty, quite uninhibited and now rightly famous junk-dealing family of Larkins.

and

A LITTLE OF WHAT YOU FANCY

A choice of Penguins

THE CATCHER IN THE RYE
J. D. Salinger

The Catcher in the Rye, Salinger's famous first novel, is a comic and touching story about a raw American adolescent. Holden Caulfield, a sixteen-year-old, relates in his own words the story of what happens when he runs away from his expensive boarding school and wanders round on his own in New York.

What does a boy in his early teens think and feel about his teachers, parents, friends, and acquaintances? Why does he want to break away from his social and domestic environment? There is no theme more typical of the present age than this, and Salinger presents it with vigour, precision, and refreshing wit.

'A real book, with its roots in living; untidy, witty, painful and pitiable' – *News Chronicle*

'Odd, tragic and at times an appallingly funny book with a taste of its own' – *New Statesman*

THE MEMBER OF THE WEDDING
Carson McCullers

'Carson McCullers has a great poet's eye and mind and senses, together with a great prose writer's sense of construction and character ... I have not been so excited by any book for years' – Edith Sitwell.

With an infinite delicacy of perception and memory, with a warmth of humour and pathos, Carson McCullers spreads before us the three phases of a week-end crisis in the life of a motherless twelve-year-old girl. Within the span of a few hours the irresistible, hoydenish Frankie – twin-sister, surely, of Mick Kelly in *The Heart is a Lonely Hunter* – passionately plays out her fantasies upon her elder brother's wedding. Through a perilous skylight we look right into the mind of a child torn between the yearning to belong and the urge to run away.

WHAT MAISIE KNEW
Henry James

'One of the most remarkable technical achievements in fiction. We are shown corruption through the eyes of innocence that will not be corrupted. Maisie is a child who must lead her life between her divorced parents, who are immoral and irresponsible. The entire action is presented through Maisie, through her developing consciousness and understanding' – Walter Allen in *The English Novel*.

THE DEATH OF THE HEART
Elizabeth Bowen

Elizabeth Bowen is without doubt one of the greatest twentieth-century writers, who combined, among other qualities, a sense of humour with a fine, scrupulous gift for divining human motivations.

The Death of the Heart is probably her masterpiece. In it she deftly and delicately exposes the cruelty of cold and conventional people of fashion when sixteen-year-old Portia comes to live with her wealthy half-brother and his wife, Anna, in London during the thirties. Portia, tormented by the agonies of her first love-affair, is obsessed by the feeling that people are laughing at her: on discovering that Anna has been reading her diary she takes a sudden explosive step which pulls everybody up short.